TROPHY WIFE

VICTORIA MATTSEN CRIME SERIES
BOOK 1

IFEANYI ESIMAI

ShotReads

eISBN: 978-1-63589-781-4

Print ISBN: 978-1-63589-782-1

Hardcover ISBN: 978-1-63589-783-8
Cover design www.coveredbymelinda.com

Published by

ShotReads, an imprint of

Ciparum LLC

270 Sparta Ave., Suite 104, PMB 152

Sparta, NJ 07871

Get a FREE copy of The Rookie!

Join my Newsletter for updates, giveaways, teasers, and a FREE copy of the prequel - The Rookie. Click here or scan the QR code.

For Chinwe...Always.
The wind beneath my wings.

ACKNOWLEDGMENTS

My heartfelt gratitude goes out to my family and friends, whose unwavering faith in me fueled this project from the very start.

I also want to extend a special thanks to a group of incredible individuals whose generous spirit has made an indelible impact on this project, and for that, I am forever grateful.

Erik S
Nneka Anaebonam
Craig Martelle
Jenn Davidson
Chinwe Anyamele
Obioha Emezie
Renee
Okechukwu Obua
Romeo Richards
Ikenna Emeghara
Charles Onunkwo
Adaeze

Every one of you has helped shape this journey in your own unique way, and I couldn't be more thankful. Your support has not only made these books a reality but has also inspired me as I continue to tell Detective Vikki Mattsen's story.

To all the readers, thank you for inviting Detective Vikki

Mattsen into your lives. It's been a joy to share this adventure with you.

Here's to the stories yet to be told.

PROLOGUE

Eve Appleton wasn't a beauty in a classic way, but something about her made men want to possess her at all costs. She never hesitated to use what she had to get what she wanted—and considered herself the luckiest woman, dead or alive.

She checked her reflection in the passenger-side visor mirror as the powerful German machine came to a smooth stop in front of the picturesque cabin.

The driver killed the engine.

Eve watched a blue jay land on the manicured lawn. An American robin hopped amongst the rainbow explosion of irises. A cardinal stood under a cherry blossom tree, waiting for its next snack. Their combined chirping and the *tick-tick-tick* of the coupe's engine as it cooled sounded like a welcoming committee.

Eve smiled, closed her eyes, and inhaled. The earthy odor from the lake reminded her of happy times with her aquarium as a little girl and conflicting times as a grown woman. The mixed emotions solidified the cabin's mysticism as the ideal romantic getaway.

The driver opened the door to step out.

Eve stopped him with a firm hand on his thigh. "Where do you think you're going?" Her voice was hoarse, smoky, and feminine.

His leg froze in mid-air. "Ah, we're here. Shouldn't we... turn it off?"

Eve took off the black jacket of her skirt suit and tossed it to the back seat. She opened another button of her sky-blue blouse.

His eyes followed her hands.

She focused her big round eyes on him through blonde peekaboo bangs that had fallen over her face. "Don't you love a little danger?"

He sighed, brought his leg back into the car, and shut the door. "Someone might see and tell."

"The caretaker has the day off."

"In that case, let's continue inside," the man said.

They entered the cabin and found themselves making love in the master bedroom.

Eve looked at the wall clock. "We still have more than an hour. We could—"

"No, no, no," the man said, not waiting to hear her suggestion. "We've tempted fate. We don't want to slap her in the face, too."

Eve swung her long legs off the bed. "Okay, I'll be right back."

"I'll come with you."

"Nope, you stay right there." She waved a finger at him. "Get your energy back. You still have work to do."

"I love it when you talk dirty."

Eve made a claw and bared her teeth. "Roar."

He laughed.

Naked but for her stilettos, she exited the bedroom and walked down the corridor to the closet that contained her husband's fishing rods and other fishing paraphernalia.

Eve opened the door. Her gaze fell on the yellow tackle box. She grabbed the handle, lifted it, and placed it by the side. Then she picked up the rectangular metallic contraption.

A *beep-beep-beep* sound came from it.

Eve frowned. "What the...?" She put the contraption down.

The beep became steady. Comparable to a hospital heart monitor displaying a flatline after a patient has passed away. Something had gone wrong.

Eve's pulse raced. A strangled whimper escaped her throat. She turned to flee. But it was too late.

The blast ripped through the air, sending her soaring. Heat seared her skin. Pain exploded in her head, neck, and face. Then everything went dark.

CHAPTER ONE

"Wow, you look worse than before you went on vacation, Mattsen!"

Vikki's head snapped up. "Thanks, Gomez. Good to see you too." She shrugged off his remark. Ten years ago, she'd strutted her stuff on the runways of Paris. Some of her colleagues called her Runway because of that stint. She was confident in her appearance.

She stopped and smiled at the uniform standing in front of the stairs to the cabin. He pushed the crime log in front of her. Vikki signed it and hesitated at the time slot.

"Twelve-twenty p.m.," the uniform said.

She nodded her thanks, wrote the time, and handed back the log.

Gomez pointed at a stack of CSO crime scene overalls on a table beside the officer.

Vikki groaned. Good thing she'd left her jacket in her car. Unconsciously, she grazed the leather holster tucked into her waistband housing her Glock 19. Reassured, she picked up one CSO and stepped into it. Pulling it over her cream-colored pants and a white blouse, put together in haste after the captain's call interrupted her well-deserved sleep.

Last night, she'd gone to the bar at an upscale hotel two towns away in Milton Township and picked up a one-night stand. She couldn't let the last night of her staycation go to waste.

Mike Gomez, her partner and a fifteen-year veteran of the St. Ives Police Department, stood at the top of the stairs, grinning. He could pass as Marlon Brando in *The Godfather*. Gomez hoped to retire next year so he and his wife could travel the world.

"Just kidding," Gomez said. "Let me guess. Your wake-up call came from Captain Levin himself?" He didn't wait for an answer. "He called me, too. Said to let you know you're the lead on this one."

Vikki nodded. "What do we have?"

"Come with me."

She entered the cabin. Rustic wood furniture, plaid fabric upholstery. Huge antlers hung above a large stone fireplace. It had a cozy feeling. But a faint smell of burned rubber and electric fire in the air, distorted the relaxed image she'd created in her mind.

"It would have been an open-and-shut case—the husband did it," Gomez said. "But it's a bit confusing. The owner's wife visits the vacation cabin, and she's blown to pieces."

Vikki stopped. "Like...blown to *pieces*, blown to pieces?"

He turned into a corridor. The acrid smell got stronger. The paint on the wall was peeling and dark in some areas.

Gomez pointed. "Exactly what I said."

A naked woman lay on the bloody floor, facedown at an odd angle. Her back was a bloody mess of torn flesh. Clear white bone protruded from one leg. Vikki's stomach tightened. Would she ever get used to this?

Gomez read from a notebook. "The vic is Mrs. Eve

Appleton, twenty-eight, wife to multi-millionaire, Preston Appleton. She was found by the housekeeper, Mrs. Enid. She said she heard an explosion around ten a.m. from her quarters in the back. She lives in a smaller cabin about a stone's throw from the back of this cabin."

"What happened to her clothes?"

Gomez cocked his head. "She was found in the buff. Her clothes are in the bedroom."

Vikki knew of explosions from gas leaks. That's why New Jersey Gas has a mantra that says call before you dig. But this was indoors. "Any smell of gas?"

"No, New Jersey Gas confirmed there are no leaks in the area."

"NJG confirmed that?"

"Yep, heating for this cabin is oil, not gas."

"Maybe she was using a propane tank and it exploded?" asked Vikki. Glass crunched under her foot. She stooped down and scrutinized a piece of plastic about two inches long. She bagged it as evidence.

Gomez shrugged. "We also retrieved a cellphone and wallet with six hundred dollars cash and credit cards from the nightstand in the bedroom."

Vikki nodded, crossing out petty robbery as a motive. "We'll have to get the crime scene unit, CSU, to figure out what went boom. Where's the housekeeper?"

Gomez led the way to the kitchen. A woman in her early sixties with graying hair sat on a chair holding a mug of something hot with both hands. She wore an old faded robe and stared into space.

"Mrs. Enid?" Gomez said.

The woman glanced up slowly and stared at Vikki with watery eyes.

"Mrs. Enid, I'm Detective Victoria Mattsen. I know my

partner has already talked to you. Is it okay if I ask a few more questions?"

Mrs. Enid nodded. "Eve was so full of life." She was hesitant, her voice a whisper.

"I'm so sorry for your loss," Mattsen said. "How long have you worked for your employer?"

"I took over after my husband died, five years."

"Did you know she was coming to visit?"

"No, I didn't know," said the old woman, shaking her head. "Mr. Appleton was supposed to be here the day before but canceled at the last minute. Maybe she just drove in to get something. I'm only informed when it's an extended stay, like for the weekend."

Vikki cocked her head. Apart from the police cruisers and Gomez's unmarked car, no other vehicles were at the premises. "How does she normally get here?"

"In her car...she drives herself," Mrs. Enid said. "One of those Mercedes sports cars that the top comes down."

Vikki turned to Gomez. "Maybe she used Uber, or someone dropped her. There's no Mercedes outside. Has Mr. Appleton been notified?"

Gomez nodded. "He's in Boston on business. He's expected back today." He headed for the door. "I'll have one of the uniforms pull Eve Appleton's data from DMV and put out a BOLO for her car."

"Mrs. Enid, what were you doing before you heard the explosion?" Gomez asked.

"Me? I was on a video call with my daughter and grandchildren. They said: Nana, what was that loud noise?"

"What time was that?" Vikki asked.

Mrs. Enid hesitated. "I'd say around ten a.m."

"Detective Mattsen...Gomez," said a uniform, poking his head into the kitchen. "You have to come and see this."

CHAPTER TWO

The window curtain was drawn, and the room made dark. A forensic technician turned on a black light.

There were fluorescing spots all over the room—the headboard, on the sheets, the floor, the walls. Vikki knew what it was but let the tech explain. It was a vacation lodge. What else do people do on vacation?

That also confirmed what she was thinking. Someone else was here with her, and it didn't seem like it was a burglar.

Gomez made the sign of the cross. "Even on the walls—Sodom and Gomorrah."

"All the glowing spots and smears are semen," said the technician. "Probably came from multiple...men...donors who had sex in this room." He pointed to a few dots on the floor. "But these are fresh. Please, follow me."

Gomez chuckled. "Fresh."

Vikki followed him down the corridor to what remained of a closet, now a smoked ruin. The tech paused at a concentration of fluorescing spots by the closet entrance.

"You think she stood here?" asked Vikki, pointing at the fluorescing dots. "Then the explosion threw her back."

"What a way to go," Gomez said.

From Vikki's periphery, someone came into view—a white coverall, gray hair, brown skin. Vikki recognized the medical examiner. She walked over. "Good morning, Dr. Patel."

"Detective Mattsen, good afternoon to you."

"Amitab, do you have a time of death yet?" Gomez asked.

"I'll say between seven a.m. and ten a.m., based on temperature and lividity."

Vikki raised the evidence bag. "I found this next to the victim. Any idea what it might be?"

Dr. Patel extended a gloved hand—flipped the bag over a few times. "Can't say for sure." He pointed at the side of Mrs. Appleton's head. "Something struck her at the side of the head, fractured her skull. I'll have more information once I get her to the lab."

"Thanks, Doc," Gomez said and faced Vikki. "Any particular thing you need me to look into?"

"We'll have to start digging," Vikki said as she headed toward the kitchen to finish up with the housekeeper. "Check CCTV on businesses on the way, or even private homes in case they caught something. Look into her financials. You never know. We want to know who was with her and who last saw her alive."

In the kitchen, the housekeeper sat where they'd left her.

"Mrs. Enid," Vikki said. "Did you see or hear anyone else in the house with Mrs. Appleton?"

Mrs. Enid shook her head. "I didn't even know Mrs. Appleton was visiting until I got here from my cabin to investigate the explosion."

"Are propane gas cookers stored in the closet?" Vikki asked.

"No, unless it's something she brought in with her," said Mrs. Enid. "That cabinet was mostly used for Mr. Appleton's fishing rods. He loves to fish when he visits. The barbecue grill is outside."

Vikki remembered seeing the tarp-covered grill when she'd walked in. She'd check it on her way out. "Does Mrs. Appleton always visit with Mr. Appleton or with other people?"

Mrs. Enid took a sip from her mug. "She sometimes comes with Mr. Appleton and sometimes alone." She put her cup down and twiddled her thumbs. "Like today, I wouldn't have known who came if it wasn't for the explosion." Her voice cracked. She took a deep breath and exhaled. "Sometimes I see that the bedsheet had been slept on, and I wasn't told anyone was coming. I mind my business. I put fresh ones."

Vikki nodded. Sometimes the owner, or someone with access, used the property as a pay-by-the-hour motel activity. "Can you think of anyone who would want to harm Mrs. Appleton?"

The housekeeper shook her head. "No."

Gomez's phone rang He raised a finger. "Gomez." He listened, repeated an address, then hung up. "A white convertible matching the description of Mrs. Appleton's vehicle was found abandoned on the street close to the Rockaway Mall."

Vikki raised an eyebrow. "Rockaway Mall?"

"Close by," said Gomez. "Do you want to handle that? I'll catch up with you—lead detective."

CHAPTER THREE

Vikki left the crime scene. A bird swooped down on the lake's surface and grabbed a fish. "Nature at its best," she murmured. "Not murder."

She sniffed the air and was surprised she got the faint smell of flowers, not the acrid smell from inside. She got in her white Ford Explorer and admired the manicured garden. The property was a nice getaway hidden on the outskirts of St. Ives.

Vikki's phone rang. Angela Baxter flashed on the screen. She placed it on the magnet holder on her dash.

Angela Baxter was a journalist with the *St. Ives Examiner*. They'd met two years ago when their orders had been swapped at the local coffee shop. They'd started talking and became fast friends. Today, they helped each other without compromising their investigations.

When Vikki was getting stonewalled by locals while investigating the death of a St. Ives high school student from a drug overdose, Baxter, who'd grown up in the town, had helped her gain the trust of witnesses.

In return, when Baxter was working on a story about a

chemistry teacher turned illicit drug industrialist, Vikki told Baxter which rabbit holes were dead ends and which ones were worth digging deeper into based on what the police knew.

This quid pro quo brought to justice a meth lab drug distribution ring that had shattered the lives of many innocent young people in their county and beyond.

Vikki tapped the screen. "Hello, Angie."

"Thank God you answered!" Baxter spoke a mile a minute. "I was scared you would extend your vacation. How was it? Don't answer that! Tell me you're on the Appleton case."

Vikki chuckled. "How did you hear about it?"

"I'm a news hound. My ears are on the ground. So, are you?"

"Yes, I'm on the Appleton case."

"Is she dead for real?"

"I'm afraid so. There was an explosion at their cabin. Did you know her?"

"Not personally, but her story was on everyone's lips when she married Preston Appleton five years ago. She, a twenty-three-year-old college student—"

"Oh," said Vikki. "Scandalous."

"He, a sixty-seven-year-old millionaire."

Vikki laughed. "He robbed the cradle."

"No, Eve raided the retirement home!"

Vikki signaled and got onto the road. "Well, that's what relationships are all about. You have what I like, and I like what you have—let's make a trade."

"You know their story?" Baxter asked.

"Nope. But I know you're itching to tell me."

Baxter laughed. "Eve and her fiancé at the time had gone to Atlantic City with their savings to bet big. Make enough to fund their wedding. They had been vocal about it at the casino. They lost it all. Preston happened to be at the casino and heard about their plans and predicament. He was cocked and primed like a Derek Jeter or A-Rod, waiting for the pitcher."

Vikki laughed. "So, the millionaire made a move on her? Kicking a brother while he's down?" She stopped at a light. Should she use the siren and lights to get there faster?

"Not really. He offered the couple one million dollars to borrow Eve for the night."

"Oh shit," Vikki said slowly. "Let me guess—they took the deal. But the millionaire loved the honey pot so much he decided to keep it."

"Exactly! But Eve also agreed to be kept. Now she's dead."

"So, what happened to the fiancé?" asked Vikki.

CHAPTER FOUR

Vikki realized the ex-fiancé had a motive too. This was an angle she hadn't considered. "Nothing is more delicious than revenge served cold."

"He moved on," Baxter said. "Last I heard, he relocated to Seattle, got married, and put New Jersey behind him." There was a pause. "So, you think the husband did it?"

Vikki sighed. "Remember, nothing goes to print until I give the go-ahead."

"Of course."

"We think someone, not her husband, was there with her. The husband's alibi is solid. He's away on a business trip. But it looks more like an accident. We have to wait for forensics. Whoever was there with her fled the scene with her car. We issued a BOLO, and the car was found abandoned at Rockaway. I'm on my way there now."

"Hmm, maybe I can meet you. I'm just exiting the mall. Give me directions."

Vikki obliged. "Please stay in your car until I get there, okay?"

"Yes, ma'am."

Vikki chuckled. "Don't call me that. I'm not your mother."

Angela was twenty-eight to her thirty-one.

Minutes later, she approached a white Mercedes convertible sandwiched between two police cruisers with flashing lights on a lonely stretch of road. No homes or businesses around. A red BMW 3 series was parked behind one of the cruisers, and a uniform was talking to the driver.

Vikki rolled her eyes. Baxter was seeking attention already. Eyes on her rearview mirror, she made a U-turn. She parked behind Baxter's car.

Once out of the car, the sun greeted her. She would start heating up in minutes. As expected, passing cars slowed. The drivers had that 'glad it was you and not them' expression.

The uniform talking to Baxter glanced up when Vikki approached. She flashed her shield and introduced herself.

"It's a pleasure meeting you, Detective Mattsen," said the uniform with black hair. "We checked the car out before we got distracted." He tipped his head toward Baxter's car.

"She's with me," Vikki said. "But she stays in the car for now."

Vikki returned to her car and retrieved blue latex gloves and evidence bags from her glove compartment. As she walked past Baxter's car, she said, "Ms. Baxter, please remain in your vehicle."

Baxter raised both hands. "Okay, okay."

Vikki peeked in through the convertible's window—saw nothing out of the ordinary. She opened the door, and it felt like opening the lid of a bubbling pot of water. The smell engulfed her—heat and rubbing alcohol. Someone didn't want their prints found. She hoped they hadn't vacuumed, too. Any fibers they found could come in handy.

She checked the back seat. Nothing. She peered under the driver's seat—too clean. Something caught her eye.

Vikki pushed the button to slide the seat back. She turned on her phone's flashlight. Sticking to the side of the console was a piece of rectangular plastic about the size of a cellphone screen.

Vikki knew what it was. The rigid plastic packaging on new screen protectors. A fingerprint magnet. She bagged it.

Vikki extracted herself from the car and bumped into Gomez behind her.

"When did you get here?"

"Just now. Find something interesting?" Gomez asked, blotting his forehead with his palm.

Vikki handed him the bag. "We should get this to forensics. I hope it's not the victim's prints on it." She glanced around. More flashing lights and more uniforms on the scene. "Everyone is here already."

Gomez took the bag. "Appleton's plane landed at Morristown airport. He said we can meet him at his mansion."

Vikki nodded.

Gomez handed the evidence bag to Detective Maria Santiago, who had just come out of one of the cruisers. She'd just made detective and was eager to learn the ropes and prove herself. She was partnered with Sean McClane, another detective in the department who didn't see eye to eye with Vikki.

Vikki and McClane went back a long way. He was a field training officer when she was a rookie. He made unwanted advances toward her, and she'd kneed him in the crotch *real* hard. Sent him to the hospital. Now he jumped at every opportunity to make her look bad. One of these days, she would take matters into her own hands before he put a bullet in her back. Gomez's voice brought her out of her reverie.

"Let's go see the husband."

CHAPTER FIVE

Gomez rode with Vikki to see the victim's husband. For about ten minutes, they drove in companionable silence. Then Gomez broke it.

"You think whomever she was getting action from did her?"

"At least took her car," Vikki said.

Vikki made a left turn as they headed to The Appleton Estate. "I think something went wrong, and whoever was there fled. Dumping the car that far and wiping it down suggests they desperately don't want to be identified."

"Maybe there's a criminal angle we haven't figured out yet."

Vikki remembered no money or credit card was taken, and the car was abandoned. She didn't see the burglary angle. "Until we hear more from the ME and CSU, it still looks like an accident to me. Speaking of the ME, is Dr. Patel on some diet? If he is, it's working."

Gomez chuckled. "If I lose that much weight in such a short time, my wife will have me screened for cancer." He ran his hand along his gut. "The good news is Patel is a doctor and knows what's best."

"Do you know how Mr. and Mrs. Appleton met?"

"Does he know how I met my wife?" Gomez said.

Vikki ignored his sarcasm. "I heard it was some kind of indecent proposal like in the movie."

"Typical! Anything with indecent in it never ends well. Just like money taken out of an ATM around two a.m. It's never put to good use."

Vikki came to a halt in front of a wrought-iron gate with intricate designs. The gate was attached to a brick fence. She wondered if the high brick fence encircled the property. "How do we get in?"

Gomez pointed at the intercom on a platform that extended like a mailbox.

"I thought it was the mailbox." She pushed the button on it.

A British-accented voice said, "How can I help you?"

"Detectives Mattsen and Gomez here to see Mr. Appleton."

There was a mechanical sound, and the gates swung inward.

Vikki drove up the long driveway to the gilded-era-style mansion on top of a hill. "This is what I call wealth."

Gomez snorted. "It's always easier to make more money when you start with a few hundred million left to you by Daddy. The rich always get richer."

"Don't hate," said Vikki, bringing the vehicle to a stop in a parking area close to the main entrance.

They got out of the car and headed for the door.

"Celebrate the man," Vikki said. "Some others have squandered millions left to them."

Vikki pressed the bell. A deep, rich chime, like a church bell, reached them. A preamble of the luxury they could expect inside the home. She admired the ornate wooden door with abstract carvings as they waited.

A uniformed butler opened the door. "Welcome. Please follow me."

Vikki recognized the British accent from the intercom at the gate. He led them to the sitting room. The foyer alone was as large as Vikki's apartment.

The room he put them in had wood-paneled walls, leather chairs, and couches that wouldn't be out of place in a museum. Only to be admired while you sat somewhere else.

The butler offered them water and coffee. They both accepted water. He brought two bottles and retreated. Moments later, firm and steady footsteps echoed in the hall-way, getting firm and confident as they got closer. The owner stepped into the room.

"Sorry for keeping you waiting. I'm Preston Appleton."

The voice belonged to an older athletic man in a dark tailored suit. He could easily be six feet tall and carried his frame well. His piercing blue eyes complemented his steel-gray hair.

Vikki and Gomez got to their feet.

"I'm Detective Mattsen—my partner, Detective Gomez. Sorry for your loss."

Mr. Appleton shook their hands. "Thank you. Please sit." He lowered himself onto the leather chair opposite them.

"Eve was so full of life." His eyes drifted from Vikki to Gomez. "I heard it was some kind of explosion." His lips quivered. "I hope she didn't suffer."

Vikki watched him. He had the mannerism of someone who had an idea of what had happened but was scared to have it confirmed. "We're still investigating, sir."

Mr. Appleton narrowed his eyes as if thinking. "It couldn't have been a gas explosion. The cabin uses oil."

"The gas company said the same thing," said Vikki. She

didn't want to be the one breaking the news to this man that his wife was probably cheating on him. But she had to. "Mr. Appleton, does your wife normally visit the cabin alone?"

"It depends. Sometimes we invite people over to swim or for a picnic. We have Mrs. Enid there, there's never a need to bring the butler." Mr. Appleton raised an eyebrow. "Why? Was someone else...hurt?"

Gomez leaned forward. "No, sir. Just routine questioning. What type of vehicle does your wife drive?"

"A white Mercedes convertible."

"And she drove it to the cabin?" Gomez asked.

"I should think so. Her car isn't here right now. You didn't see it at the cabin?" His eyes narrowed. "Detective, what are you getting at?"

"Sir, your wife's car was abandoned by the roadside in Rockaway."

"Rockaway? My God. Was it a burglary that went bad, and she was murdered?" He shook his head. "There was an explosion. No, it doesn't make sense." Suddenly, the tension left his face. "Was she... Could she have been having an affair?" His voice was a low monotone.

Vikki exchanged glances with Gomez. "We're still investigating. What's her routine like? Where would she have been around ten a.m.? We're trying to figure out the last person who saw her alive."

"The butler must have seen her this morning," said Mr. Appleton.

Vikki's insides tightened. She hoped Mrs. Appleton had spent the night at home. Soon, the butler appeared. He must have been summoned through a hidden button. Or had he been listening in?

"Paul, what time did Mrs. Appleton leave in the morning?"

"Her usual time, sir. Around seven a.m. She drove herself. I presume she left for the office. Is something wrong, sir?"

Mr. Appleton lowered his head and sighed. "There was an accident at the cabin—an explosion." His eyes glistened with tears. "Eve is gone."

Even in grief, the butler tried to remain composed. He took a deep breath and let it out as a sigh. "I'm so sorry...so sorry for your loss, sir." His voice cracked, but he pulled it back in. "Madam was nice and generous."

Mr. Appleton nodded. "You can go, Paul."

Vikki didn't speak until the butler was gone.

Mr. Appleton noticed and said, "That's Paul Smith. He's been with me for a long time. He's like family. He's trained in physical combat, and I trust him with my life. After all, he has three opportunities to kill me every day when he serves me food."

Vikki didn't speak. She took a sip to buy time until Mr. Smith's footsteps faded. "So, people must have seen her at the office?"

"Yes, of course," said Mr. Appleton. "A few weeks ago, Eve said she wanted to learn more about the company, so I handed her over to Adam. Mr. Adam Rinkin, one of my executives—my Chief Operating Officer—to bring her up to speed. He knows everything."

"Where can we find Mr. Rinkin?" asked Gomez.

"At the office. I'll call to let him know you're coming."

"It's not necessary," said Vikki. "Surprise is always a good thing. We'll introduce ourselves."

Mr. Appleton looked at her a second longer and nodded.

Vikki got up. "Again, sorry for your loss. Depending on where our investigation takes us, we might be back to follow up with you."

A business card appeared in Mr. Appleton's hand. "Please

call me if you need any assistance. No stone should be left unturned to get to the bottom of this."

The butler appeared again. Vikki was sure there was a button. He showed them out.

Gomez shook his head as they headed for Appleton Inc. in the next town. "Wow, a multimillionaire cuckold? I thought I'd seen it all. I wonder what Mr. Rinkin has to say?"

"Our ETA is twenty-five minutes," said Vikki. "We'll find out soon."

CHAPTER SIX

Appleton Inc. was tucked away in the woods. The building was rectangular, with clear glass walls and steel beams. From the car park, it resembled a spacecraft that had landed in the woods with offices inside.

Vikki and Gomez strolled in. In the reception area, pictures and models of their real estate holding adorned the walls and display cases.

Gomez flashed his badge at the receptionist. "We're here to see Mr. Rinkin."

The pretty blonde with large eyes swallowed. "Do you have an appointment?"

"No, it's police business," Vikki said.

The receptionist picked up the phone.

Moments later, a man in his mid-thirties, dressed in a tailored navy blue suit, strode into the reception and approached them. "I'm Adam Rinkin."

Vikki introduced them and said, "Is there a place we can talk in private?"

Mr. Rinkin raised an eyebrow. He hesitated. "Sure, my office. What's this about?" He led the way down a corridor.

Vikki did not answer. They went up a short flight of stairs and entered an office. He shut the door behind them, sat on one side of a mahogany table, and pointed at two seats on the other side.

"We spoke with Mr. Appleton about thirty minutes ago at his home," said Gomez. "And he said we should talk to you. He mentioned you're helping Mrs. Appleton understand the Appleton business better. What exactly is that?"

Mr. Rinkin smiled, nodding. "Mostly the real estate deals we have. The process of finding suitable locations for commercial or residential purposes. I haven't seen her this morning, though. She's a devoted and eager learner. But, some days, she takes her time getting here."

Vikki studied a framed picture of Mr. Rinkin with a brunette and two girls about six that could pass for twins. She refocused on Rinkin.

"Unfortunately, she won't be making it today or ever," Vikki said.

"What do you mean?" Rinkin asked.

Vikki pursed her lips and sighed. "There was an explosion this morning in the Appleton's' cabin by the lake. Mrs. Appleton lost her life."

The color drained from Mr. Rinkin's face. "What?" His voice was a whisper. "What happened?"

Gomez cleared his throat. "All we know now is there was an explosion."

"My God...Eve is dead?" Mr. Rinkin sank into his seat.

"Did she call this morning to say that she would be running late?" Vikki asked.

Rinkin removed his cellphone from his pocket. His fingers shook when he tried to tap the screen. He hid it by doing a piano riff with his fingers before tapping the screen again. "Hmm, she...she didn't text or call."

He placed the phone on the table and picked up a pen. He

tapped the cap against his lips and bit down on it now and then.

Vikki wondered why he was so nervous. Maybe shock. "Is there anyone you know she hangs out with?" she asked.

Rinkin gnashed his teeth on the pen's cap. "I-I don't know. She normally meets me here in the office with a cup of coffee. And sits where you're sitting now."

"So, she goes to Starbucks every morning?" Gomez asked.

"I guess so. Maybe not Starbucks, but another brand."

Vikki leaned forward. "Has she ever mentioned going to the cabin before coming here? Or hanging out with anyone in the few weeks you've been coaching her?"

Rinkin shook his head. Beads of sweat sprouted like corn seedlings on his forehead. "I can't say for sure. I never ask... she's the boss's wife." He let out a nervous laugh. "When she's late, she's late. I'd assumed there was a line at the coffee shop. It's not like I'm going to give her the third degree."

Gomez took out a small notebook from his jacket pocket. "Where's this coffee shop?" He tapped his pocket and made a show of searching for something to write with. "Can I borrow your pen, please?"

Rinkin dabbed his forehead with tissue and gave Gomez a pen. "I don't know. The closest one is by the strip mall not far from here."

Gomez nodded and wrote in his notebook. "I'm going to ask you a few routine questions. Where were you around ten a.m.?"

Mr. Rinkin pursed his lips. "Around ten?" he thought for a moment. "I went to the car wash, then came to work." He laughed. "I park under a chestnut tree at home. Birds take dumps on my car all night long."

"Do you have a receipt?" Gomez asked.

"A receipt?" Rinkin drew a blank.

"For the car wash," Gomez said.

Mr. Rinkin patted his pockets. "No, I have a subscription booklet—my wife bought it for me when I threatened to chop down the tree." He let out a nervous laugh. "It's in the car."

Gomez chuckled. "Happy wife, happy marriage."

"Exactly."

"Which car wash was that?" Gomez asked.

"The one on Main Street. *Clean* something."

Gomez finished scribbling, then glanced at Vikki. "Any more questions?"

Vikki got to her feet, shaking her head. "Thank you for your time, sir, and sorry for your loss." She handed him her business card. "If there's anything you remember, please don't hesitate to call."

Mr. Rinkin stared at the card. He appeared distraught, as if the loss was only just sinking in.

"Don't worry, we'll find our way out," Vikki said.

Once in the car, Gomez opened the Explorer's glove compartment and brought out an evidence bag. He dropped Rinkin's pen inside it. "I couldn't resist. It has fingerprints, sweat, and saliva on it. Just in case we need his DNA."

On the drive back to the office, Vikki went through the events so far in her mind. A woman was dead. She was probably having an affair. Someone who witnessed her death was at large.

Gomez blew out a breath. "What do you think about Mr. Rinkin? You think he's dipping his pen in his boss's ink well?"

Vikki laughed. "I can't say for sure. He was genuinely shocked when we broke the news. We'll let the evidence guide us." She signaled and turned into the police department's parking lot.

CHAPTER SEVEN

St. Ives Police Department was located at the end of Main Street, next to Town Hall. Vikki parked in her designated spot. She got out of her car and headed into the building.

To get to the elevator, she must pass the reception area on the ground floor close to the entrance. And you couldn't avoid a chat with Jody.

"Hello, Vikki! You're back!"

The voice belonged to Jody Allison, the department's administrative secretary. She smiled from behind her desk.

Vikki wrapped her arms around her shoulder.

"My favorite French runway model. You look pretty as ever. I still don't know why you stopped being a model to chase around murderers."

Vikki smiled. Many years ago, while in college in France, she'd done a little modeling. When she'd joined the police academy, some friends had found out and called her Runway. At SIPD, Jody had got wind of it.

"I'm still waiting for your go-ahead to introduce you to my nephew. You two would make beautiful babies!"

Heat rushed to Vikki's cheeks. She couldn't think of a comeback.

"How was your vacation?"

"It was a staycation. Got some much-needed rest."

Jody was sixty-five and widowed. She loves to dress in bright, colorful print dresses with her usual patterned sweater over them. SIPD and her cats were all the family she needed to keep going. She'd been at SIPD longer than everyone else and knew everything. She was the person to talk to if you had questions about the police department or needed favors.

"Hi, Gomez? How's my girl Serena?"

"Nagging as ever," Gomez said and headed for the detective squad room.

Jody shook her head. "Men. So, you got a good rest?"

"And read, too." Vikki's mind drifted to Ted, the man she'd met at five-star hotel two towns away. She let out a sigh. He was one of the best in a long time.

Ted had not disappointed. So much so that she'd thought she might extend her vacation and have him one more night. Ted was inclined to it, too, but no. She was a veteran of one-night stands. It was not a strategy for getting to know you better or starting a relationship. Sorry, Jody. No can do for your nephew.

Vikki had gotten home as the brilliant sky was doing an orange, yellowish transformation. She'd barely slept a few hours when her cell phone had rung.

"Vikki, Vikki!" Jody snapped her finger.

"Hmm?"

"Stop daydreaming. You can tell me all about it later. Captain Levin wants you to drop by his office once you come in. I think forensics got back with their findings. It seems like what happened at the cabin was no accident."

Vikki blinked. "Really? Thanks, Jody." She headed for the chief's office.

CHAPTER EIGHT

Vikki knocked on the door—poked her head into the captain's office. "Good—"

"Mattsen! Come in." Captain Levin's voice sounded like crinkled wrapping paper.

His outfit, consisting of a navy blue suit, white shirt, and red tie, was a constant. His shirt and tie he changed daily. You could tell by the color and design, but his suit was always navy blue. Same one? It was anyone's guess. His gray hair was combed and neat. He looked more like a CEO of a small business.

Vikki sat in one of the seats opposite the captain. She hoped this wouldn't drag. The chairs were uncomfortable. It wouldn't take long for her ass to go to sleep.

"Vikki, we must get to the bottom of this as soon as possible. I just got off the phone with the mayor. Mr. Appleton is a high-value constituent. The mayor wants whoever was behind this apprehended as soon as possible. I spoke with CSU—they think a pressure cooker bomb was what killed Mrs. Appleton."

Vikki frowned. "A cooker? Why—?"

She was about to ask why they were cooking inside a closet and stopped. "Like the Boston Marathon case."

Captain Levin nodded. "Exactly. Anyone with an internet connection can put one of these together. I want answers, like yesterday."

"Evidence from the scene suggests Mrs. Appleton could have been having an affair. When a wife is murdered—"

"Yes, yes, the husband is good for it. But he was more than two hundred miles away."

"Maybe he hired someone to take care of it. Sir. As an HVC, his net worth is north of eight figures. Rich people never get their hands dirty. Perhaps it was the person who was with her."

He raised his hands, palms out. "That's what I need *you* to find out. Remember your rookie year in New York?"

"Yes, sir. Follow the evidence to wherever it may lead, HVC or not?"

"It's no different for this case, too," he said.

She turned to go.

"Vikki," said the captain. "I hope you didn't spend your vacation looking for answers. You're still a detective, even when you're on vacation. No vigilante activities. The law still applies."

Vikki nodded. She knew exactly why Levin had uttered those words. Twelve years ago, her entire adoptive family had been brutally murdered, and Levin was one of the officers who had responded to the 911 call. Consumed by the desire for revenge, Vikki had turned to Levin for guidance. He had convinced her to join the police academy and learn the skills needed to track down and apprehend criminals.

"I know, sir," Vikki said. She left his office and walked to her desk in the detective squad room.

She groaned. In her absence, her desk had been used as storage for files. She was tempted to dump them in the trash.

"Welcome back, Vikki," said John Wan, a colleague. "Oops! They did it again," he said in his best Britney Spears imitation. "I'll help you." He picked up some of the folders and carried them to the break room.

Vikki picked up the rest and followed. "Thank you." She couldn't believe Gomez had let that happen. They dropped the files at a table in the break room.

"Anytime, Vikki," said John.

Just as she settled in, Gomez walked in holding a piece of paper. "I dropped off Rinkin's pen with the crime lab to run his fingerprint and DNA through CODIS after it was analyzed."

CODIS is the national database of DNA profiles from convicted felons and evidentiary samples. Vikki knew that unless Rinkin had committed a crime in the past, there was no reason for his DNA to be there. "You think he was once a felon?"

Gomez shrugged. "You never know. But once they've analyzed it, we can run it against DNA recovered from the scene. What did the chief want?"

"The explosion was no accident. Someone planted a pressure cooker bomb in the closet."

"You're shitting me," Gomez said."

"I shit you not. Similar MO to the Boston Marathon bomb years ago."

Gomez cocked his head. "Correct me if I'm wrong. It's rigged to a timer to detonate it, right?"

"That can work," Vikki said. "Anyone could have set the bomb. They didn't need to be in the area to detonate it. It could've been activated using a cell phone attached to it. The perp calls the number and boom."

"Nice. The question now is, who wants Mrs. Appleton dead?" He raised the paper in his hand. "Mrs. Appleton's financials. She's a frequent flyer at Starcoffee on Red Oak Street. Stops there every morning. She likes to shop, too. Macy's, Nordstrom, Sears, Amazon, you name it."

"Really? I thought it was Starbucks, according to Rinkin."

Gomez shrugged. "It gets better. I just spoke with Santiago. She showed a picture of the victim at the coffee shop."

"Where did she get the picture from?"

"From Mrs. Appleton's Facebook profile. Get this. Not only did one of the baristas recognize Mrs. Appleton, but she directed her to a manager who she said was 'friendly' with Mrs. Appleton. His name is Joe Hulland."

Vikki couldn't believe the turn of events. "Well, let's go pick up Mr. Joe Hulland then."

"Wait! There's more!"

Vikki smiled. This was getting better.

"Santiago brought Mr. Hulland in. And guess what, his fingerprints matched those recovered from the plastic you found in the Mercedes."

Vikki crossed her arms over her chest. "No way." Her eyes narrowed. "Are you pulling my leg? A welcome back joke?"

"Yes way," Gomez said. "They just finished processing him. Should be brought in here soon."

Vikki's phone rang. She raised a finger. "Mattsen," she answered.

"Detective, Dr. Patel. Do you have a minute?"

Whenever the ME asked if you had a minute, he'd found something interesting. "I'll be right there." She turned to Gomez. "Your pal has something interesting to show us."

"Amitab? Christ! I don't even get to sit down. This case has now started to move at the speed of light."

Vikki got out of her chair. "That's exactly what the

captain wants, a quick resolution." She looked around and caught John Wan's eyes. "John, please ask Santiago to put the suspect in a free interview room when they bring him in. We need to dash over to the ME's lab."

John gave a thumbs-up. "Will do."

CHAPTER NINE

The ME's office was across the courtyard from the police department. It could also be reached through an underground tunnel.

The municipal building was to the right, which also housed the court. And to the left was the correctional facility. Any official business with the town could be conveniently handled in one general location.

Gomez pulled open the door to the building with Medical Examiner written in bold letters on the entrance. "After you."

"Thank you," Vikki said and stepped in. She braced herself. She could never get used to the presence of death and the smell of embalming chemicals. The smell hung around like a ghost in all the morgues she'd been to.

Gomez grumbled as he took a disposable shoe cover and jumpsuit from the shelf. "The people are already dead. Why can't we walk in?" He raised a leg and hobbled on one foot, trying to slip the shoe cover over his shoe. He did the same for the other foot before stepping into the overall.

Vikki felt the same way as Gomez but kept it to herself. Moreover, he knew better, too. It was necessary attire to prevent contamination of Eve Appleton's body. She dressed quickly and walked in. Dr. Patel, in full protective garb, leaned over a female body on the autopsy table.

It was Eve Appleton, cleaned up. Her injuries resembled different-shaped potholes on a newly tarred road. Her torso spotted a Y-shaped baseball-stitched scar. Starting from both shoulders, meeting at the top of the sternum and extending down to her pubic region.

"Mattsen and Gomez," Dr. Patel said, glancing up from his patient, his voice strained.

Vikki swallowed. He had peeled Eve's face off her skull. It resembled turning a sock inside out. She'd never get used to this.

"What do you have for us?" asked Gomez.

"The lady had a blunt force trauma to the skull. Possibly the pot cover flew off and fractured her skull. She took the full impact of the explosion. I only saw injuries like that with soldiers during wartime. The time of death remains between nine-thirty and ten-thirty a.m. Death was swift. Under her nails were clean. Nothing came up on the pubic comb. She didn't have any hair down there in the first place. However, a strand of black hair was retrieved from inside her vagina."

Vikki got excited. For one, Mrs. Appleton was blonde. Secondly, DNA could be recovered from hair samples. "Was it a complete sample with follicle?" She regretted her words just as they came out. Dr. Patel had been doing this since she was in diapers.

Patel gave her a 'don't be silly' stare. "Of course. The follicle must be there for it to be usable. I've sent it to the lab for analysis. There was no bruising either. Intercourse before the blast appears to be consensual. The recovered DNA is being analyzed."

Gomez rubbed his hands together. "That's great. This case might be a slam dunk after all. We should also collect samples from Mr. Hulland. If positive, that should put him at the scene."

Dr. Patel shrugged. "There you go. It is now up to you guys to figure out what happened."

To Vikki, the picture still wasn't clear. "Let's go talk to Mr. Hulland. Maybe he can shed more light on motive."

CHAPTER TEN

"I only interact with the lady with the Benz when I hand over her coffee through the little window," John Hulland said.

Mattsen and Gomez sat opposite Mr. Hulland in interview room one at the police station.

Twenty-five-year-old John Hulland in business casual—tan chinos and a light-blue shirt, looked like Brad Pitt in *Thelma and Louise*.

Gomez nodded. "Really! You've never been in her car. Or the cabin by the lake?"

"Nope, I swear. What would I be doing there? All I serve is coffee."

Vikki smiled. "So, what were your fingerprints doing in her car?" She raised a picture of the evidence bag with the screen protector in it.

Mr. Hulland stared at it, bug-eyed. He opened his mouth, then shut it. He took a deep breath and exhaled through his mouth. "Detective, why don't you ask the owner of the car? She'd be in a better position to tell you." His eyes darted from Mattsen to Gomez. When they said nothing in response to his suggestion, he said, "Did something happen to Eve?"

Gomez raised an eyebrow. "I thought you didn't know her."

"I have to write her name on the cup. That's how I know her name. She tips well, too."

Vikki was tired of playing cat-and-mouse games. "Mr. Hulland, early this morning, there was an explosion at her cabin, and Mrs. Appleton lost her life."

John Hulland sprang to his feet. "Mrs. Appleton is dead?"

"Yes. And someone was with her when she died. We suspect foul play." Gomez pointed at Hulland. "Your fingerprints were in her car."

Vikki threw in some fear tactics. "Once we confirm the DNA found in her belongs to you, you will go away for a long time. The sooner you start talking, the quicker we can find ways to help you help yourself."

Gomez shrugged. "Or we'll slap you with murder." He paused—stared at Hulland. "Why did you do it?"

"Murder? I didn't do anything." Beads of sweat dotted Hulland's forehead. "All I did was sleep with her. Why would I want to kill Eve? She rocked my world."

Vikki and Gomez exchanged glances.

"How did you meet?" Gomez asked.

Hulland exhaled. "I served her coffee one day, and she said I reminded her of her ex-boyfriend. I was about to finish my shift, and she said she would wait for me in the parking lot." Hulland appeared confused. "I didn't expect to see her, but she was there. She said let's go for a drive in her car. I thought it was a joke. We drove to a dark corner, and she sucked me off."

"Vikki was skeptical.

"Just like that?" Gomez asked.

Hulland raised an eyebrow. "Yeah, just like that. I couldn't believe it either! Then she would pick me up now and then. We'd go to the cabin, too."

Vikki glanced away like she was uninterested. But inside, her mind was doing cartwheels. *At least we're getting somewhere.* He'd put himself at the cabin.

"Or we go do it in the car," Hulland continued.

"Do what?" Vikki asked.

Hulland rolled his eyes. "Fuck."

Shaking his head, Gomez said, "Yeah, right. Because you have a magic cock? So, what happened this morning? Did she tell you it was over? You got angry and blew her up?"

"No!"

"Where were you this morning at ten a.m.?"

"In...in the coffee shop. It was my day off. But someone called in sick, and I was called in."

"Very convenient," said Gomez.

Vikki knew they were barking up the wrong tree. It didn't sound plausible that he would murder a pretty woman who'd picked him up to have some fun with. Hulland agreed to have his cheeks swabbed. That said something.

Vikki cut him loose. "Don't leave town without checking with us."

She had a uniform drop Hulland off.

"I think he was genuinely shocked to learn about Eve," Vikki said.

Gomez chuckled. "Yes, but we've seen stranger things. The motive is my main concern. Maybe he doesn't have any reason himself. A pretty rich woman—heck, who spits out sugar when it's thrust into their mouth?"

Vikki shook her head. "Men."

Gomez wagged a finger. "But, if he was promised money to do her, then that's a whole different kettle of fish. Her husband has already done a similar thing before. I mean, spending a lot of money to get what he wanted."

Vikki saw the rationale behind that. "Good point. We'll pull his financials. But why would she pick up random men to sleep with?" As soon as the words left her mouth, she wished she hadn't uttered them. She did the same thing. Luckily, Gomez didn't catch on.

"I don't judge. People do things for reasons that make sense only to them. Me, I follow the evidence."

Vikki sighed. "We're back to square one. The motive for murder is not there for the barista unless he's being financially motivated by someone."

Gomez's phone rang. "I'll check his finances. If the evidence leads to him, then a jury of his peers will have the opportunity to determine his fate." He took out his phone. "Gomez."

Vikki watched as Gomez's features went from concern to surprise to unbelievable.

"Are you sure?" There was a pause. "I'm so sorry. Of course, you're sure." He nodded. "Okay." He finished the call and turned to Vikki. "You won't believe this."

Vikki raised an eyebrow. "Try me."

"Two different DNA were recovered from her. One was from the barista and the other from Mr. Rinkin. Also, the DNA from the strand of hair found in Mrs. Appleton matched the DNA recovered from Mr. Rinkin's pen." Gomez waggled his eyebrows. "Getting the pen was a genius move. Right?"

Vikki tapped her lip with a finger. *What was going on here?* "If I remember correctly, he said something about birds pooping on his car and having to go to the car wash."

"That's what he said. But he was somewhere else sharpening his tool. Why don't we send some uniforms to pick him up? I'll check his alibi with the car wash. He might be charged with obstructing a police investigation, too."

Vikki was at her desk when she was informed that Rinkin had been brought in. She got a bottle of water from the vending machine and headed for the interview room.

CHAPTER ELEVEN

Vikki stopped at the one-way mirror outside the interview room and watched Mr. Rinkin.

His poker face was as perfect as his tailored suit. But his right hand gave him away. It shook like crazy. He placed one over the other. Both trembled. He slipped them into his pocket.

Vikki took a deep breath and walked into the room, followed by Gomez.

The odor of Rinkin's cologne, sweat, and something she'd smelled in other scared people filled the room.

Mr. Rinkin's eyes came up. There was a slight quiver in his lips. "W-why am I here? I-I thought we were done. Why did you send uniformed police to the office? Do you know the embarrassment you caused me?"

Vikki placed the bottled water in front of him. "Mr. Rinkin, I don't want to know."

"We have a few questions for you," Gomez said. "This time, we want the truth."

Rinkin's eyebrows knitted together. "W-what do you mean, the truth?"

"You lied to us," Gomez said.

"I was at the car wash. You can ask them."

Vikki shook her head. "We did, and they assured us you were there, but—"

Rinkin threw out his hands, palms up. "So, what's the problem?"

Gomez cocked his head. "Why don't you tell us?"

Rinkin raised both hands. "There's nothing to tell."

Vikki inhaled and let it out in a rush through her nose. She'd accessed the DMV database. "Let's see. Yes, here it is. A white Lexus LS is registered to you, and a white Tesla is registered to Lisa Rinkin of the same address as you. Your wife, I presume?"

Rinkin opened his mouth, then closed it again without saying anything.

"Let's say you drive your wife's car sometimes," Vikki said. "So, which car did you wash this morning?"

Rinkin's eyes darted from Vikki to Gomez.

"Think carefully," said Gomez. "I spoke with the manager at Speedy Car Wash. He said some nice things about you. We also found a piece of hair inside Mrs. Appleton. I'm sure your wife would love to know who it belongs to and where it was found."

Rinkin shut his eyes tight like he was trying to wish the whole thing away. He opened them. "Please keep my wife out of this."

"Your wife is the least of your problems," Vikki said. "Mr. Rinkin, a woman is dead, and evidence suggests you were the last person to see her alive. The car you brought to the car wash was Mrs. Appleton's Mercedes—what happened? And start from the beginning."

Vikki glanced at the ceiling. The camera's light was on. Even though Rinkin was not under arrest, she thought it would be better to read him his rights now.

"Mr. Rinkin, I know you're very busy, and I don't want to drag you from your office again. I'll read you your rights, just in case." She pointed at the camera. "This session will be recorded, too."

Mr. Rinkin inhaled and exhaled, his shoulders slumping as he emptied his lungs. He nodded. "Okay."

She Mirandized him. It took a moment. Then Rinkin opened up.

"It was about a month ago or six weeks ago," Rinkin said. "Preston called me into his office."

"Preston, as in Preston Appleton?" asked Vikki.

He nodded. "Mr. Appleton wanted me to teach Eve...Mrs. Appleton, about Appleton Inc. She wanted to know everything. I asked him why. He said it was Eve's idea. After all, if anything happened to him, Eve would be better off if she understood the business."

Rinkin took the water bottle, cracked it open, and took a long drink. "There wasn't much to teach. Preston had inherited a few buildings from his father. He used them as collateral to borrow from banks. He purchased run-down and distressed properties and developed them into offices and housing complexes in New York City and the five boroughs. With luck and rezoning, most of the buildings went up in value. He borrowed more and expanded."

"Okay, nice and good," Gomez said. "So, how did the affair start?"

Vikki bit her tongue. Gomez should know better. You didn't interrupt a suspect who was already talking.

Rinkin exhaled. "It was informal. I would explain the process to her. We would go out for lunch, come back, then she would leave. One day, she needed to pick up something from the cabin after lunch. She was driving, so I had no say in it. At the cabin, she cornered me. She said she found me attractive and asked if I found her attractive?"

Rinkin took another sip of water. "I said, of course. Then she told me about how she met Preston. But, over the years, she'd realized she was only a conquest for him—another project. Once a task was finished, he lost interest. She had become a completed project. It had been a long time since anyone cared for her."

Vikki pursed her lips. She gave a heavy nod.

"I...I told her I was happily married," Rinkin said and chuckled. "She said so was she. But it shouldn't be a deterrent. Before I knew it, we were making love by the lake."

Now that he was in the talking mood, Vikki knew she had to bring it to the present. She was surprised he hadn't asked for a lawyer. "Okay, so what happened this morning?"

CHAPTER TWELVE

Rinkin rubbed his nose and tugged at his collar. His eyes darted from Gomez to Vikki, then down to his interlocked fingers. "Eve sent me an email this morning—she wanted us to go to the cabin. Normally we went during lunch, but this time she wanted us to go first thing in the morning. You have to understand I was completely under her spell. I met her in the parking lot of the coffee shop. We drove to the cabin."

"What time was that?" Vikki asked.

"We were at the cabin by nine."

Vikki scribbled on her notepad. "What happened next?"

Rinkin ran his fingers through his hair. "We made out in the car, ended up in the master bedroom, and had sex. Then... then Eve, Mrs. Appleton, said she'd be right back. She left the bedroom—walked down the corridor."

"Did you know where she was going?" Gomez asked.

Rinkin locked eyes with Gomez, then looked away. "No."

"What was she wearing?" asked Vikki.

Rinkin paused—stared into the distance for a second. "Just high heels."

She nodded. "Please continue."

"I heard the closet door creak open. Seconds later...I heard an explosion." Rinkin's voice cracked.

A few beats passed as he composed himself.

"Do you know what exploded?" Gomez asked.

Rinkin shook his head.

"What happened next?" Vikki asked.

"I screamed her name and rushed down the corridor. There...there was blood everywhere. She lay there on the floor, not moving. She had a bleeding gash on her head. I froze where I was." Tears streamed down Rinkin's face.

Vikki exhaled. "You didn't call nine-one-one?"

"I panicked. Her eyes were wide open...just staring. I checked for a pulse even though I knew she was dead. I returned to the room, put on my clothes, and left with her car. I collected my thoughts on the way. I was sleeping with my boss's wife. She'd just been blown to bits. I didn't want my wife or my boss to find out. The first thing that occurred to me was to wash the car. Get rid of any evidence. I took the car to the car wash."

"You did a poor job," Gomez said. "You forgot to clean the room. You left man syrup in the room, on the floor, and the big daddy of all, a strand of hair in her."

Rinkin just stared.

"Is that the whole truth and nothing but the truth?" Vikki asked.

Rinkin's lips quivered. He clasped a shaky hand across his mouth.

Vikki couldn't wait anymore for him to make up his mind. "Look, Mr. Rinkin, Mrs. Appleton was killed by a bomb. A pressure cooker bomb."

"A bomb?" Mr. Rinkin said.

Vikki fixed her eyes on him. "Someone placed that bomb there. And right now, you're the only person of interest. If there's anything you know, tell us now."

Rinkin's eyes went wide. He turned as white as a ghost. "My God. Do you think someone wants me dead, too?"

"You tell us," Gomez said. "What do you know?"

Rinkin exhaled. "A few days ago, I thought a car was following us as we drove to the cabin from the coffee shop."

Gomez sat up. "Color, make, and type?"

"I think it was blue. A Chevy Malibu."

Adrenalin rushed through Vikki. Suddenly, she was alive again. "Can you describe who was driving it?" she asked.

Rinkin shook his head slowly.

"Take your time," Gomez said. "Think."

"No, it had tinted windows."

Gomez leaned back. "Is that all you have? So, it was just a random blue Chevy. Do you know how many blue Chevvies are in St. Ives? Let alone New Jersey. It would be like looking for a needle in the proverbial haystack."

"Wait." Rinkin dug into his pocket. He brought out his phone. He tapped on the screen a few times, then swiped with his fingers. He held up his phone. It was a photo of the front of a blue car taken at a distance. The license plate wasn't completely clear.

Gomez glanced at Rinkin, his lip parting. "No shit." He took a picture of Rinkin's phone. "I'll see if the guys at forensics can do anything with the plate number, then I'll check with DMV." He got up to leave.

"One second, Gomez," Vikki said and left her seat.

"Can I leave now?" Rinkin asked.

They both ignored him and stepped out.

Vikki exhaled. "What do you think?"

"He ran from the scene of an accident, destroyed evidence, and lied to us," Gomez said. "Let's book him."

"He hasn't asked for a lawyer," Vikki said. "He would once we detain him. And the lawyer would say he left the scene because he was shell-shocked and scared."

Gomez let out a breath. "Let's search for this blue Chevy and see where that leads."

They went back in.

"You're free to go," Vikki said. "Cancel any vacation plans. We might need to talk to you again. I'll have one of the officers drop you off."

Rinkin raised both hands, shaking his head. "No, thank you. Enough police for one day. I'll take an Uber."

Vikki walked him to the exit when the car arrived. Who had been following Eve and Rinkin? What had happened to Eve Appleton? She passed the admin again on her way back.

"Vikki, the captain wants to see you," Jody said and raised an eyebrow. "Déjà vu, right?"

Vikki smiled.

CHAPTER THIRTEEN

Vikki sat opposite Levin in his office.

Captain Levin made a steeple with his fingers. "You're telling me that Mr. Rinkin, the COO, was sleeping with the CEO's wife?

"Yes, sir."

"And he was there when the bomb went off?" He shook his head. "He'll have a lot of explaining when his wife finds out." He waved his hand dismissively. "That's his problem. But there seems to be something else going on?"

"I think the bomb was planted by someone who wanted to send a warning and not necessarily kill."

Levin's gray eyes narrowed. "Explain."

"The Boston Marathon bombers wanted mass casualty. In addition to the explosive material, they loaded the pot with nails, ball bearings—things that could maim. It was not so in this case."

"I see what you mean. But at the end of the day, we have a homicide. We have to find out who put the bomb there. Keep me updated."

That was the captain's dismissal. Vikki left his office and went in search of Gomez.

"Mattsen! We're in luck," said Gomez as soon as he spotted Vikki. "The blue car is a rental. An Edward Brandon picked it up from Newark Liberty airport five days ago. Hasn't been returned yet. I've put out a BOLO. Hopefully, something will bite sooner than later."

At the mention of a bite, Vikki's stomach rumbled. She looked at the wall clock. "It's already five p.m. I'm famished. I'm going to grab something."

"Where? The corner store? It doesn't matter. I'll come with you. I'll tell Santiago to reach us if something comes in from the BOLO."

There wasn't a line at the corner store close to the police station. Vikki ordered a six-inch roast beef wrap with hot and sweet peppers, American cheese, lettuce, red onions, and tomatoes.

Gomez stared at Vikki's order. His Adam apple bobbed up and down "Nice. I want the same."

"Swap the beef for the chicken, and Serena will be extremely proud of you."

"Make it one foot," Gomez said.

Vikki laughed. "Now you've spoiled it. Are you trying to make her a widow?" She headed for an empty table. "Do you want to eat here? Or take it back to the office?"

Gomez smiled. "We have a free table. I want to eat in peace. We'll enjoy our food and put it away quickly without distraction."

Detective Santiago came up to Gomez and handed him a piece of paper once they entered the squad room. "This just came in. The blue Chevy was located in front of fifteen Speck Street. The property belongs to Mrs. Agnes Brocker, a seventy-year-old widow."

A surge of adrenaline rushed through Vikki. "Did they make contact with the driver?"

Santiago shook her head. "They were told not to engage."

"Good," Vikki said. "Ask them to remain unseen and follow if the car moves. We'll be there soon. We don't want to spook him." She smiled. "Thank you, Maria."

"Don't mention it." Maria looked around and said in a low voice, "McClane gets uptight whenever I mention you or say I'm doing something for you. Is there something I should know?"

Vikki laughed. "An incident from when I was a rookie that he's still keeping a grudge about. But don't forget he's your supervisor."

"I know, but that's a long time to be mad. Anyway, I'm glad I was able to help." Santiago left.

Vikki made a mental note to stop asking her for favors. She turned to Gomez. "Let's go."

CHAPTER FOURTEEN

Vikki and Gomez arrived on scene within fifteen minutes.

Gomez waved to the officer as they passed him.

The house was on a cul-de-sac. Number fifteen was at the end. It was a Cape Cod-style one-story with the typical large central chimney. Lights were on, and it seemed like someone was home.

The Chevy was in the driveway. Vikki parked behind it. The car wasn't going anywhere. She was glad the sun had set. Most of the houses had lights on—the neighbors were indoors. In case it got dangerous, she didn't want any collateral damage.

"Let's go," said Gomez.

Vikki brushed her finger against her holster as she approached the entrance. She felt reassured.

Gomez rang the bell.

There was a muffled *ding-dong* from inside. They waited. Nobody came.

Vikki knocked and reached for the door handle. "You think nobody's home?"

Gomez shrugged, his right hand hanging close to his holster.

Vikki turned the knob. The door was unlocked and creaked open with a gentle shove. "Hello! SIPD! Anyone home?"

Vikki eased it open and walked in. Her Glock was in her hand, pointing down. The door opened into a short foyer that led to a living room. Her heart thudded.

The living room was an open floor plan with granny-chic furnishing—floral wallpaper, pillows on all the couches in the living room.

The dining table was circular with straight-back chairs. Little framed pictures hung on the wall, from black-and-white photographs to colored ones. Some were placed on the shelves and tables. They documented the life cycle of a couple and a girl over the years.

Vikki cocked her head. Mozart's *Eine Kleine Nachtmusik* drifted down the hallway. It could be coming from one of two closed doors.

Gomez nodded and led the way, his gun drawn. He turned the handle of the first one and pushed it slowly with his foot.

The room was dark. Photos hung on lines, held up by pegs —a darkroom.

Vikki leaned closer to the pictures. She couldn't believe her eyes. They were all pictures of Eve Appleton. She was coming out of a white car. Shopping, then in different compromising poses with men.

Vikki recognized Adam Rinkin and John Hulland—having sex with Eve Appleton. Jesus.

It was like someone was collecting evidence for a show-down in court.

Mattsen and Gomez whirled to the flushing of a toilet. It came from the door next to the one they were in.

Vikki cursed. They should have secured the house first

before investigating. The photos had surprised them. She held her Glock in a two-handed grip with the barrel pointed down. She stepped out of the darkroom and stood in front of the toilet door. There was a click, and the knob turned.

The door opened, and a tall black man with an athletic build wearing just shorts stepped out. The man's eyes widened. "What the—?"

Gomez lifted his gun. "St. Ives Police Department! Raise your hands—and keep them up!"

"What's going on?" said the man, raising his hands. His voice was deep and confident. He shuffled back a few steps. More surprised than concerned.

Gomez continued to yell. "Are you Edward Brandon? Is that your blue Chevy outside?"

"Yes, and yes!" said the man. "What is this all about?" His eyes darted from Gomez to Vikki, then fixed on Vikki.

Vikki blinked. There was something familiar about that voice—that body.

The man's eyes narrowed. "But the car is—" His eyebrows shot up. "You!"

Gomez flashed his badge with his left hand and raised his gun higher. "Interlock your fingers behind your head! You're under arrest for the suspected murder of Eva Appleton!"

Edward Brandon's head jerked to face Gomez. "Murder!" He shook his head. "No, no. You have the wrong person."

"That's what they always say," Gomez said. "Keep them up."

Vikki groaned. Recognition slammed into her like an eighteen-wheeler running a red light. That face, that body—belonged to her one-night stand at Milton Township.

CHAPTER FIFTEEN

Vikki and Gomez were back in the police department with Edward—Ted. She kicked herself for not linking the names. But she didn't know his last name. Who was the idiot who first shortened Edward to Ted? Couldn't they have taken a cue from names like Alexander or James? Simple Alex and Jim.

Vikki whispered in her partner's ears. His jaw all but dropped to the floor.

It took a moment for Gomez to process the info. Then he said, "In the biblical sense?"

Vikki nodded.

"Wow, no shit," Gomez said. He was silent for a moment. "The captain is not going to like this." He let out a breath. "I'm sure you'll need a moment or two. I'll bring him to the station with the uniform outside. So far, he's not giving any trouble."

Vikki was back at the PD. She'd had time to think on her drive over. She would explain to Levin and excuse herself from the case. He would understand. He'd guided her since she'd joined the force ten years ago in the aftermath of Alexis' and her dad's murders on St. Patrick's Day. He was the closest thing to a father figure she had.

Vikki knocked on the captain's door and stepped in.

"Mattsen! What can I do for you? I was about to call it a day," said Levin. "Why the horse face?"

Vikki didn't know how to say it, but it had to be said. Better she brought it up than the perp.

She took the seat on the other side of his table—looked him straight in the eyes. "Em, last night...I was with the man we brought in. I think somebody else should handle the interview."

It took Levin a few seconds to deduce the situation. "You are dating him?"

"No, not like that. Last night I saw him at a bar in Milton Township. We...kind of hit it off and ended up in his hotel room."

If her boss was judging her, he hid it well.

Levin shrugged. "Well, it is what it is. You have a job to do, and I don't think it will cloud your judgment. I have full confidence in you."

Vikki's lips parted. She felt an unexpected release of tension. "Thank you, sir."

"Now go dig deeper into the story. We must get to the root of this."

She left the office and headed for the interview room.

Gomez stood by the interview door with some papers in his hands. "What did Levin say?"

Vikki shrugged. "He said to carry on. I have full confidence in you."

Gomez nodded. "I agree with him. I dug into the perp's profile. He's Edward Brandon, MD, a forensic pathologist. His permanent address is in Duluth, Minnesota."

Vikki stopped in her tracks. Last night he'd said he was in medical services and was afflicted with wanderlust—a strong desire to travel. She'd envisioned more of a medical equipment sales rep. "A doctor? What was he doing with all those photos?"

"Beats me. I guess we'll have to ask him. But there's more."

Before Gomez could say anything, Vikki opened the door and walked into the interview room.

Gomez followed.

Ted was in shorts and a white button-down shirt. He looked relaxed with both elbows resting on the table. Where was she going to start? Maybe the captain was wrong. All she could think of was Teds firm body hovering over her last night. *Awkward.*

Ted smiled and waved. "Hello, Vikki. I thought you guys had forgotten me."

Vikki thought a formal introduction should be in order. "Well, Dr. Brandon, I'm Detective Mattsen, and my partner, Detective Mike Gomez."

"Please, call me Ted."

Vikki pulled out a seat opposite him. "What were you doing in fifteen Speck Street with several compromising pictures of a woman—the subject of a homicide investigation?"

Ted raised an eyebrow. "Homicide! Mrs. Appleton murdered? What happened?"

Gomez rubbed his hands together and leaned forward. "Doc, we ask the questions. Maybe you can tell us? We have a suspect who can identify you as having been following Mrs. Appleton around."

"Where were you this morning between nine and ten a.m.?" Vikki asked.

Ted stared at her as if contemplating what to say. Finally, he said, "Remember last night? I was asleep in the hotel room recovering. I checked out just after noon. You can verify with the hotel's housekeeping and reception. I never left until they woke me up. You wore me out."

Even though it was out in the open, heat rushed to Vikki's cheeks. She lowered her head. It would have been worse if she hadn't given Gomez a heads-up.

Vikki raised her head. "I'm glad I rocked your world. But you still haven't answered the question. Why were you following Mrs. Appleton?"

CHAPTER SIXTEEN

Ted sighed. "I'm a licensed private investigator with the state of Minnesota. I rented the Airbnb for a few weeks and was hired to do a job here in St. Ives."

"Who hired you? And to do what?" Gomez asked.

Ted cocked his head and gave a Cheshire cat smile. "Mr. Appleton, of course. He hired me to follow his wife and take pictures." He took a deep breath and expelled it noisily through his nose. "Pictures of her in compromising situations."

Vikki knew that divorce was on the horizon once one spouse had a PI taking pictures of the other.

Gomez tapped a finger to his lips. He exhaled and said, "There are good local PIs here. Why hire from MN?"

"I guess you'll have to ask Mr. Appleton. But I think people also like that I'm a forensic pathologist. I tend to think outside the box. Two for the price of one."

"But wouldn't that affect your job as a doctor?" asked Vikki. Then she remembered the wanderlust thing.

"I moonlight. I move from one temporary job to another."

Gomez nodded. "So, have you presented your findings to Mr. Appleton?"

Ted shook his head. "Not yet. I was supposed to, but he sent a text at the last minute. He was going on a business trip, and I should suspend all surveillance until he returned. So to relax, I went to the hotel."

"Which hotel was that again?" Gomez asked.

"The Hilton in Milton," Vikki and Ted said simultaneously.

"Oh," Gomez said and slid out of his chair. "I'll be right back."

Vikki sensed this was another dead end. But they now knew that Mr. Appleton was suspicious of his wife. Could he have murdered her out of jealousy?

She remembered her childhood. Both parents had been junkies. Her father had abused her mother repeatedly. There are more than one reason spouses could murder each other.

"Vikki? Vikki."

A voice pulled her out of her reverie, and she refocused.

"Are we done?" Ted said.

Just then, Gomez walked in. He exhaled. "Vikki, the hotel confirmed his alibi. Unless he's Spider-Man, he couldn't have left the hotel without them knowing."

She nodded. "Yes, you're free to go."

Ted got up. "Listen, if there's any way I can help, don't hesitate to ask. How did Mrs. Appleton die?"

Gomez shook his head. "Pressure cooker bomb."

Ted's eyes widened. "A bomb? You should have the FBI looking into it."

"No," Vikki said. "The feds like to take over things."

"And take credit, too," Gomez said, shaking his head. "No way, Dr. Minnesota Nice. Thanks for your suggestion. It's our job, our town. We'll solve it."

"But thanks, though," Vikki said.

They locked eyes.

"Can you give me a ride back to my place?"

"Nice try, Romeo," Gomez said. "Come on. I'll give you a ride." He turned to Vikki. "I'll call it a day after I drop him off. See you tomorrow?"

Vikki sighed and nodded.

They all left the interview room. Gomez walked out with Ted. Vikki went back to her table in the squad room. The skeleton crew for the night was arriving. What would have happened if Gomez hadn't volunteered to take Ted home? She didn't trust herself being alone with him. But why?

Her phone rang. She glanced at the screen and groaned. It was Baxter.

"Hi, Angie. Sorry for not getting back to you. It's been hectic."

"I can imagine. Do you have anything I can use for tomorrow's paper run?"

"Hmm...we don't have anything solid. This is off the record." Vikki told her about the ME's findings. The barista, Rinkin, and Ted. She didn't mention she'd slept with him the night before.

"That makes sense," Angie said.

Vikki was alert. "What makes sense?"

CHAPTER SEVENTEEN

"Remember how Mr. Appleton and Eve hooked up?" Angie said. "The indecent proposal?"

"Yes." Vikki got up and straightened some files on her table.

"So, I tracked down the ex-fiancé."

Vikki stopped what she was doing. She kicked herself for not thinking of that. She headed for the exit.

"He works for a computer company in Seattle. I left a message in the morning and told him there was an accident and Eve Appleton had lost her life. He called me back."

Vikki waved to Jody at the reception area, exited the building, and got in her car.

Angie laughed. "He said her loss saddened him, but he didn't sound like he was. I sensed blood in the water and pounced. I asked him if the breakup was amicable."

Vikki let the car's Bluetooth take over the phone audio. "What did he say?"

"Oh boy—what didn't he say!" Angie's voice came from the car's speakers. "He said Eve came from nothing. By the time she was fourteen, she was using sex to get whatever she wanted. In college, he thought she was in love with him. But, in reality, she used him to get closer to his friends and fraternity members."

"What was special about his friends?" Vikki asked.

"You know—rich kids that come from money. The types you read about their parents in papers. She fucked them all. His words, not mine."

"Wait. Do you think he's still mad enough to come down here with murder on his mind after all these years?

"Who knows!" Angie said. "Let me finish. It gets better. He shed some behind-the-scenes light on what happened the day they met Appleton five years ago. After they lost all their money at the casino, Appleton approached with the proposal. According to Eve's ex, he'd refused. But Eve convinced him she would do it for them. She slept with Appleton. He became smitten and offered her marriage."

Vikki chuckled. "She struck gold."

"You bet. She accepted and flew away with Appleton on his private jet. Left the fiancé there in Atlantic City."

Vikki drove into the parking lot of her apartment complex. She entered the building and took the elevator up. Luckily, she didn't lose the call. "My God, did he get his million dollars?"

Baxter laughed. "I know you shouldn't speak ill of the dead, but Eve was a bitch."

Vikki laughed.

"Even though she was about to become a trophy wife, she collected the million from Appleton, gave her ex a hundred thousand, and called him a pimp. When he returned to their hometown and told his friends, that was when other stories about her came up."

Vikki was thinking fast. "Maybe she changed? Fell in love with someone new and wanted a divorce?"

"What? Didn't the ME recover two different DNA from

her—one from the barista and the other from the executive? What type of love is that? Her ex ended the conversation with, 'Eve never downgrades. She always upgrades.' Maybe karma has finally caught up with her?"

Vikki got off the elevator and walked to her three-bedroom apartment. She opened the door and stepped inside. It was good to be home. She could see the whole apartment but for the bedrooms and two and a half baths.

A leather couch, coffee table, and a flat-screen TV she rarely watched accented the sparsely furnished living area. Then the dining area and kitchen.

She placed the phone on the couch, took off her jacket, and hung it on one of the dining chairs. The circular dining table was mainly used for files and folders when she brought work back. The only thing that was used regularly was her coffee maker.

"Vikki? Are you still there?"

Vikki picked up the phone. "Yes, I just got home. I never knew I could miss this place so much after a staycation."

"Yes, it happens. So, what should I do?" asked Baxter.

"Well, there's nothing concrete yet, as you know. Maybe mention the police are following a few leads. You can mention her car. We're done with that. Call back tomorrow. If we have a smoking gun, I'll let you know."

"Have a good night, Vikki."

"Bye." Vikki hung up and placed the phone on the kitchen counter.

All kinds of thoughts bounced through her mind. She knew she was missing something, but what? Enough about work. Her mind drifted to Ted Brandon, MD. Vikki fanned herself. Thoughts of him sent a rush of heat and excitement through her.

There was a half-empty bottle of wine in the fridge. She

got a wine glass, filled it to the brim, and sat on the barstool. She should soak in the tub.

About twenty minutes later, she was soaking in her tub, thinking about the case, when the answer came to her. Eve's phone. They'd need to take a more critical look at it. Tomorrow, she would pull her phone records.

CHAPTER EIGHTEEN

Vikki arrived at work early the next day. She smelled burned coffee, turned around, and went to the coffee shop close by. She came back with two dozen assorted donuts and a box of joe from Dunkin. Nobody would go near the coffee pot until the joe was empty.

She filled a cup with black coffee, grabbed a frosted strawberry donut with sprinkles, and headed for her table.

Gomez looked up when she walked in. "Mattsen!" He smiled. "How are you?"

Vikki lowered her head and eyed him. "Why are we so upbeat?" She waited for the punch line.

Gomez shook his head. "Nothing."

Vikki thought he'd changed his mind on what he wanted to say. What else but a sly innuendo?

"The only thing we haven't gone through is Eve's phone," Vikki said. She sat and sipped some coffee. "I think the key to what happened probably lies with who she spoke with in the past few days." She told him about her conversation with Angie and how Eve was a selfish social climber and money-grubber.

Gomez shrugged. "His words against hers. Maybe we should look closely at the ex? He might still be brooding from the way she dumped him. Revenge is a dish best served cold."

"I agree. We tackle the leads in the Northeast before focusing on the Pacific Northwest."

"No problem," Gomez said. "Incoming and outgoing phone numbers and texts in the past five days or two weeks?"

Vikki tapped a finger on her lip. "Five days. We can always expand. If we don't get any leads, we can consider going to Seattle to talk to the ex-fiancé."

"How was the interview yesterday evening?" said a familiar voice.

Vikki looked up as Levin walked into the general office. "Good morning, sir!"

Levin made a sour face. "Jesus, Vikki!" He placed a hand on his chest. "I thought someone was behind me with a weapon. Stop doing that. You're going to give me a heart attack one day. Be more like Gomez, mellow—morning, Mike."

"Chief," Gomez said with a nod.

"Working on it, sir." Vikki couldn't help herself. Authority was authority, and she owed the man a lot. "The suspect was cooperative. It turned out he had legitimate reasons to be where he was. The property is an Airbnb, and he's a licensed PI. Currently employed by Mr. Appleton to gather information on Mrs. Appleton."

Levin nodded. "The wind of divorce escalating to murder? Anyway, keep me updated. I'll be back in my office." He raised a glazed donut with crushed Oreo sprinkled on top. "Thanks."

Vikki smiled. She knew it was his favorite.

Gomez sprang to his feet. "You didn't tell me you brought in donuts. I'll grab some coffee before it's gone. I'll talk to the IT guys. See if they can get her records from her phone."

Gomez left.

She exhaled noisily. She ate her donut, interrupted now and then by other staff members as they trickled in. Some raised their cup of coffee or donut to show appreciation.

Her nemesis, McClane, walked in with a donut. When he heard people thanking Vikki for the donut and coffee, he made a show of discarding his half-eaten donut on his table. When he thought no one was looking, he stuffed it into his mouth. Vikki shook her head.

It was now a waiting game. Vikki caught up on some reports from completed cases for the next couple of hours. Gomez came and went. The man couldn't sit still for long.

"Detective Mattsen." Vikki raised her head.

Santiago came over to her table and gave her some papers.

"Hi, what are those?"

"I saw Gomez in the corridor. He said he'll be a minute. He asked me to give you these."

CHAPTER NINETEEN

Vikki took the sheets of paper. "Oh, I see."

"Thanks for the coffee and donuts," Santiago said.

Vikki smiled. "Don't mention it." She glanced at the print-out. It was five days of phone calls and text messages to and from Eve Appleton's phone. She glanced through. A few were local calls, and more than half were 1-800 marketing calls.

Vikki checked the time on her phone. It was nine-thirty a.m. That was a decent enough time in the morning to cold-call someone. She'd circled some numbers on the statement starting with the local ones. She recognized some, like Mr. Appleton's and Adam Rinkin's.

The first three were a hair salon, a nail place, and a dentist. She called them to confirm. Once someone identified the business, she apologized, said, "Wrong number," and hung up. She might revisit them later to find out why Mrs. Appleton had called. The fourth was an Attorney's office.

A woman with a sweet voice answered. "Anderson's Law office, this is Monica speaking. How can I help you?"

"Hello, this is Detective Mattsen from St. Ives Police

Department. I have a few questions about one of your clients, Mrs. Eve Appleton."

There was a pause. "You said you are from the police?"

Vikki sensed her reluctance. "Yes, Detective Victoria Mattsen."

"The attorney is not in the office right now, but if you can call back in twenty minutes, he should be here by then." She ended the call.

Vikki wrote TCB— 'to call back'—against the number, then continued down the list. For a few of the numbers, the names of the phone owners appeared on the screen when it rang. She would cut it off.

Gomez walked in and flopped into his seat. "Why do people love free stuff? Even those who already came in with a donut and coffee still wanted the free one."

"You didn't get any?"

"I did, plus a second one."

Vikki rolled her eyes.

"I see you're already working on the list, any luck?"

"Not yet. But there's an attorney in Dover she'd called five days ago." Vikki checked the time on her phone. "I'm going to call him back now."

The phone was answered on the second ring. "Monica, Detective Mattsen here. May I speak with Mr. Anderson? I spoke with you earlier."

"Yes, ah…"

Why was she hesitating again? "Monica?"

"He's not back. Can I take a message?"

"Yes, tell him I'm investigating a homicide and have a few questions for him. When will he be back?" There was another pause. Vikki wondered if someone was telling her what to say.

"He's gone for the day. Can you call back tomorrow, please?"

"Okay, will do." Vikki ended the call. She turned to

Gomez. "I think the lawyer was there. He didn't want to speak to me."

Gomez raised an eyebrow. "Maybe he has something to hide?"

Vikki got up and put on her jacket. "Let's go find out."

"Dover, here we come," Gomez said and upended his coffee cup. "Maybe we should buy more coffee and donuts on the way. By the way, did you know that Dr. Brandon wears size fourteen shoes?"

Vikki shrugged, "No, why?"

Gomez grinned as he slipped on his jacket. "You know what they say about men with big feet?"

Here we go. Ah, that's what he wanted to say when she walked in.

CHAPTER TWENTY

Vikki pulled up in front of the strip mall. She scanned the shingles of the businesses, looking for Anderson Law.

"What type of lawyer has an office in a strip mall, for Christ's sake," Gomez muttered.

Vikki smiled. She was thinking the same thing. "Remember Saul Goodman in *Breaking Bad*?"

"Oh, the sleazy type." Gomez pointed to their right at an office with Anderson written over the door. "Over there."

Vikki parked in front of the office. The wall facing the parking lot was almost all glass. The receptionist was visible through the glass window. She was precisely what she'd pictured in her mind. Full-figured, about forty, dressed in a sundress with a sweater, oversized glasses, and no makeup.

Gomez exited the car. "Let's see Mr. Anderson and find out what he's hiding." He held open the office door for Vikki. "After you."

Vikki entered. The room smelled old and musty. The walls were covered with wallpaper that looked like 80's wood paneling. The receptionist sat behind a small table with a computer sandwiched between two metal filing cabinets.

"Monica?"

"Yes?"

Vikki flashed her badge and introduced themselves. "I spoke with you earlier. We're here to see Mr. Anderson."

She reached for a binder labeled 'appointments.' She flipped through a few pages, then stopped. "Do you—"

"I spoke with you about an hour ago," Vikki said, her voice stern. "Could you kindly tell Mr. Anderson that two detectives from SIPD are here to see him?"

Monica's eyes widened. "Hold on." Her voice was a whisper. She got up, strutted over to a door, and knocked once. She opened the door, glanced over her shoulder, and scurried in like a mouse pursued by a cat. Less than a minute later, she reappeared. "Mr. Anderson will see you now."

Mr. Anderson's room had the same wallpaper as the reception area. He could be a close double for Richard Gere in the movie *Pretty Woman*—double-breasted suit, premature graying at the temples.

"How can I help you, Detectives?"

Vikki didn't bother wasting time with introductions. "We found your number in Mrs. Appleton's phone while investigating her homicide. Why did she call you?"

Mr. Anderson pursed his lips. He seemed to be contemplating what to say.

Vikki knew he didn't have to tell them anything. Lawyer-client privilege. Unless he had something to do with her murder, there wasn't anything to gain by stalling their investigation.

"It's up to you," said Gomez. "We could get a warrant and work with the judge on how limited or broad it could be."

Vikki didn't like twisting lawyers' arms. Some were deft in pulling rabbits out of anything hollow.

Mr. Anderson smiled. "That won't be necessary." His

voice was oily and smooth. "Mrs. Appleton consulted me to have some questions answered."

Gomez nodded. "What type of questions?"

"They were hypothetical ones. She wanted to know if she could challenge the prenup she signed in the event of a divorce."

Vikki waved her hand in the air for him to speed things up. "And..."

"I told her it was iron-clad. She was better off remaining Mrs. Appleton."

Vikki felt like a balloon with all the air let out. She'd hoped they would find a smoking gun.

"Is that it?" Gomez asked. The disappointment in his voice was hard to miss.

Mr. Anderson raised a finger. "But, if Mr. Appleton were to die unexpectedly, she was bound to inherit, as any other spouse would, Mr. Appleton's estate."

They thanked Mr. Anderson for his time and left.

CHAPTER TWENTY-ONE

At the PD, Vikki and Gomez reviewed the information they had so far. She stood in front of the white dry-erase board they used as a murder board and canceled out the suspects one after the other.

"It seems like Mrs. Appleton was interested in divorce, too. But whatever she would get from the prenup agreement wouldn't be enough. You think that got her killed?"

Gomez shrugged. "There's a lot of money at stake. The husband could have paid someone, but I don't see the motive for murder."

Vikki shrugged. "Maybe jealousy? He found out about the barista and Rinkin, flew into a rage, and decided to terminate her."

"Thinking along that vein, that could be why he hired Dr. Brandon to take pictures. Gather evidence for a court case if she tried to challenge the prenup. As far as murderer for hire, I doubt that's in Brandon's wheelhouse."

Vikki let out a breath. She liked Brandon and preferred the clean version where he only took pictures and was not involved in a murder-for-hire scheme. "And he took the Hippocratic oath: First, do no harm."

Gomez gave her a look. "An oath has never been a deterrent to anyone intent on seeing something through."

"So, the barista we've ruled out." Vikki crossed out his name. "He was at work." She put a question mark behind Rinkin's name. "Then there's Rinkin?"

"He was in the cabin when the bomb went off," Vikki said. "Could he have instigated it and then pretended he was at the wrong place at the wrong time?"

"What was his motive?" Gomez asked.

"Maybe he wanted to end the relationship," Vikki said. "He loves his wife. Eve is his boss's wife. He found out about the barista, or perhaps he found Jesus—whatever the reason. The thrill and excitement are now gone, and he wants out. She says no way. So, he plants the bomb and kills her."

She stared at the board for a long time.

"Vikki, are you trying to set the board on fire with your stare?"

Vikki exhaled. "That would be exhilarating, at least." She shook her head. "Just trying to find some logic to this madness. I'm beginning to think that this was an accidental death."

Gomez turned to face her. "How?"

"What did the housekeeper say about Mr. Appleton visiting the cabin? Do you remember?"

"It should be in the notes, but something like she was expecting Mr. Appleton, but he canceled at the last minute."

Vikki nodded. "Okay, and the mall lawyer told us the only way she could get more money was if Mr. Appleton died rather than getting a divorce. One thing we know is that she's capable of ditching anyone."

Gomez sniffed. "So, she comes up with a plan to build a

pressure cooker bomb and blow her husband up when he visited the cabin."

Vikki cocked her head. "Yeah, it's an easy bomb to make. The blueprints and videos are online."

"Yeah," said Gomez. "But there's no evidence that she did that. Yes, she visited the mall and could have bought a pressure cooker. But her phone history doesn't show she visited any websites with the blueprint for making a bomb."

Vikki was quiet, then said, "But she could have used a computer that wasn't hers." She felt they were missing something.

"Hold on," Gomez said. He went to his desk and brought back the pictures from Dr. Brandon.

They went through them. Several photos were taken of her in the kitchen section of a department store.

"We could get a warrant for receipts to confirm the purchase," Gomez said. "She's smart. She could have figured out the bomb-making all by herself. Or maybe Rinkin or the barista helped her."

Vikki tapped her lip. "I think we can drop the barista for now. I think he was only there for the romantic entanglement. Rinkin had more to lose. His marriage and his job. Let's revisit Mr. Appleton and see if we can get our hands on Mrs. Appleton's computer. Have the IT guys dive deep and look for more evidence to support Eve building the bomb."

Gomez chuckled. "This sounds crazy. She tried to kill her husband and ended up the victim of her own device."

CHAPTER TWENTY-TWO

Vikki rang the bell. Paul Smith, the butler, opened the door and ushered them in.

In the foyer, Vikki was taken aback to see Mrs. Appleton's picture on an easel next to a sculpture of Venus. The goddess encompasses everything a woman's heart desires—love, beauty, sex, fertility, prosperity, and victory. Was Eve a villain or victim?

Underneath the photo was the caption 'Gone too soon' against a white background. An open guestbook sat on a table nearby. Vikki noticed that the last entry was Adam Rinkin.

Vikki and Gomez followed the butler to the living room and were told to wait. It didn't take long for Mr. Appleton to appear.

"Detectives, I didn't expect you back so soon. Do you have news?"

"Did Mrs. Appleton own a computer?"

"Of course. Who doesn't own one these days?"

"Some people use their phone, others an iPad, I wasn't sure. Can we borrow it?" Gomez asked. "It's going to help with the investigation."

Mr. Appleton nodded, then the space between his eyebrows narrowed. "What's this all about?"

Vikki cleared her throat. "Mr. Appleton, I'm—"

"Preston. Please call me Preston."

Vikki would have preferred to stick to his last name. "Erm, Preston...I don't know how to say this, but it seems your wife's death was an accident."

Mr. Appleton gave her an incredulous look. "The explosion was an accident? The bomb just happened to be there?"

Vikki stared him in the eye. "The pressure cooker bomb that killed your wife...was meant for you."

Preston stood. "What! How is that possible? You mean someone tried to murder me and got Eve instead?"

"No," Vikki said. "Your wife tried to murder you, and the bomb went off prematurely."

Preston sat *slowly*, his face the color of the pale Venus sculpture in the foyer. "My God. I knew we were having problems, but not to that extent." He paused for a moment. "What has that got to do with the computer?"

"We believe she must have learned how to make the pressure cooker bomb online," Vikki said. "We've already checked her phone. It was clean."

Gomez cleared his throat. "Mr. Appleton...why did you hire a PI to follow your wife and take pictures?"

Mr. Appleton did a double take. Then he smiled. "You guys are good. You made the connection." The smile faded. His features became dark. "I gave her everything money could buy, yet she wasn't happy. Eve and I grew apart. I'm... I'm sure you already know the circumstances under which Eve and I met. One thing I've learned from life is that people don't change. With enough motivation, they could try. She could do to me what she did to her fiancé. So, I hired a PI to follow her and document her movements. Just in case." He shook his head. "But murder?"

"We found the PI and the pictures," Vikki said. "I'm afraid your instincts were right."

Preston lowered his gaze. "Was Rinkin in the pictures?" He spoke in a monotone. Like he was asking for something, he didn't want to know the answer to.

Vikki and Gomez remained silent.

"Your silence speaks volumes," said Mr. Appleton. "The son of a bitch! He was here not too long ago, and he acted like everything was all right" Preston's shoulders slumped. "I was supposed to meet the PI that morning and see what he had. But something came up, and I had to go to Boston."

Vikki locked eyes with Preston, then glanced away. She felt sorry for him.

Preston got up. "I'll go get the computer." A few minutes later, he came back with a laptop.

Gomez wrote him a ticket for it. "Does it have a password?"

"I guess it should. It...was Eve's. I wouldn't know it."

"I'm confident our IT guys will get in," Vikki said.

CHAPTER TWENTY-THREE

Vikki was at her desk in the detective squad room when the IT forensic guy showed up.

"What do you mean it's clean?" Vikki asked. Her voice was sharp and loud. She was talking to the guy from the computer department in charge of forensics. She'd given him Mrs. Appleton's computer to tear apart.

"D-Detective Mattsen," James Madden stammered all long limbs and fingers. "She has two accounts on the laptop. I went through it. Then I had Johnny go through it, too. We found nothing about bomb-making. But we're working on breaking the password to the second account."

Vikki exhaled. "I'm sorry for raising my voice. I thought this was a slam dunk."

"Hey, no worries," James said and gave a high-pitched laugh. He looked around and leaned in conspiratorially. "At least you're not throwing stuff at people like Gomez."

"I heard that!" Gomez said from his desk. "Wait till I get there. I'll throw you out of this office." He sat back and sighed. "Are we back to square one?"

"I'll let you know once we break in," John said and made a hasty exit.

Vikki sat at her desk, her fingers interlocked together, thinking. She turned to Gomez. "Every other person checked out. The only person whose story had holes is Rinkin. He was there when the explosion happened. He ran instead of calling for help."

"Come on. He was screwing his boss's wife in his boss's house. There's no way he could have buttered it up to get sympathy from anyone. He came up with the best option and took it. He ran."

"I think we should talk to him again. Maybe there was something he forgot to tell us."

Gomez sipped his coffee and made a face like he was constipated. He had gotten coffee from the break room. "We should have stopped for coffee on our way back, and now I'm back to drinking bad coffee again."

"We can send some uniforms to pick him up," Vikki said.

Gomez shook his head. "No, he might decide not to come. I think surprising him at home with his wife could be to our advantage."

CHAPTER TWENTY-FOUR

Vikki rang the bell of Rinkin's house.

A beautiful woman in her mid-to-late twenties opened the door. "Hello."

Gomez flashed her a smile and his badge and introduced them. "You must be Mrs. Rinkin. Is your husband home?"

"The police? Is everything okay?" She glanced over her shoulder. "Honey, the police are here to see you."

Rinkin appeared. "Detectives! I thought we were done at the office?"

His wife whirled to face him. "Honey, what's this about?" Her hand flew to her lips. "Oh God…is it about Eve? Poor woman."

Rinkin's eyes darted about like a cornered rat.

Vikki came to his rescue. "We have a few more questions for him about Appleton, Inc."

"It's okay, Lisa. I don't think it will take too much time," said Rinkin. He squeezed her shoulder. "I'll talk to them outside."

Lisa hesitated, then nodded. She walked away from the door.

Vikki turned to Rinkin as soon as the door shut. "You're holding back on us. What exactly happened yesterday morning?"

"I told you everything I know."

"Hello," Gomez said, grinning and waving at two little girls starring at them through the window.

"It's up to you," Vikki said. "You can come clean, and we go away. Or we can haul you off to the station in handcuffs with your family watching."

Rinkin looked back at his two girls and moved away from the window.

"You knew about the bomb, didn't you?" asked Vikki. She sounded sure, but she was fishing.

Rinkin shut his eyes tight, then opened them. "Eve sent me a text to meet her at the coffee shop parking lot yesterday morning. I left my car there and drove us in hers."

Vikki was tempted to interrupt him. They already knew that. But she decided not to. He might say something new.

Rinkin continued. "We went to the cabin. I knew Preston was supposed to be there and said so. But she said he left for Boston—an emergency meeting."

"Okay," said Gomez. "What happened next?"

"That was when she now said that she had built a pressure cooker bomb. She did her research online with her laptop. The bomb was set to go off while Preston was at the cabin. But because Preston wasn't there, she needed to turn it off. I didn't believe her. I thought she was joking."

"Did she joke around a lot?" Vikki said. "Why didn't you believe her?"

Rinkin threw out his hand. "It sounded ludicrous!" His eyes darted to his house, and he lowered his voice. "When we got there—as I told you, we made out in the car and continued in the house. Then I *honestly* believed she was joking."

Gomez shook his head.

"Jesus, I mean no disrespect," Rinkin said. "She knew a bomb was there and still had time to screw?" He chuckled. "She kept on saying we had time. That was when I felt she was serious. I insisted, and she agreed to turn it off. She got out of bed and walked down the corridor to the closet. I opened the bedroom door a crack and watched her. She opened the door and stooped down. She reached for something, drew back, then the explosion came."

Vikki remembered the fluorescing evidence the CSI guy had showed them yesterday morning, giving credence to his account.

Rinkin took a deep breath and shuddered as he exhaled. "Then I heard the explosion. I rushed to her. It was terrible. I checked her pulse, and once I confirmed she was dead, I ran. I took the car to the car wash. I abandoned it along the road, walked to the next street, and hailed a taxi."

"How?" Vikki asked.

Rinkin shrugged. "With the ride app. I picked up my car from the coffee shop and returned to the office. I'd just gotten to the office when...when you showed up."

"Karma is a bitch," Gomez said under his breath, shaking his head. "Even when she tried to do the right thing, it still bit her in the butt."

Vikki was convinced Rinkin had laid it all out. He didn't want his wife to find out, but there was no way she wouldn't know. That was his problem, not hers. When you decided to have an affair, you should be ready to accept the consequences. She had one more question for him. "What time did Eve text you?"

Rinkin dug into his pocket and brought out his phone. "Yesterday morning around seven a.m." He turned his screen to show Vikki.

Vikki read the text. *Preston traveled to Boston last night. Meet at usual place 8 a.m.*

She turned to Rinkin. "And you didn't speak with her before then?"

"No."

CHAPTER TWENTY-FIVE

Vikki sat in her chair, waiting to hear from the IT guy. They were nearing a solution.

A few minutes later, James Madden walked into the office.

"If it isn't one of the apostles," Gomez said as he caught sight of him. "This is a done case. Don't tell me anything I don't want to hear."

James chuckled. "See no evil, speak no evil, and hear no evil." His smile faded when he noticed Gomez was not laughing with him. He turned to Vikki.

"Detective Mattsen, I'm done! We cracked the password. I went through the laptop's web history, and the smoking gun was laid out as if Hansel and Gretel were walking in front of me."

"We're not in your nursery rhyme class," said Gomez. "Tell us what we'd understand."

"Once inside, it was easy to follow the breadcrumbs left by Mrs. Appleton. She visited several websites with simple and clear instructions on how to make the bomb. How much damage an explosion could do depended on what you filled the pot with. Nails, pieces of metal, glass. Some throw in roadkill, like IEDs used by terrorists in the Gulf wars. When the sharp objects penetrate the body, they cause structural damage and introduce infection from decaying matter. Hard to treat."

"Yeah, but she did none of that," said Gomez. "Just a plain bomb."

"The only confusion was her choice of setting it off," said James.

Vikki raised an eyebrow. "What do you mean?"

James waved both hands in the air. "The blueprints on the website she visited showed how to activate the device using a cellphone. Call the cellphone, and it triggers the bomb. However, this one was motion-activated with some seconds delay, based on the debris recovered at the location. Once you pick it up—tick-tick-tick, then *boom*. She didn't have a chance."

"What?" Vikki asked. "Why would she then go to pick it up?"

"It's funny. It seems like she forgot she used a motion-activated trigger." He shrugged. "How can you forget that?" He shook his head. "Anyway, there it is. I have to run. If you have any questions, you can call me on my cell. We'll be playing pinball at The Bull Dog Café."

Vikki smiled. "Thanks, James. Have fun." She went to the murder board and wrote 'closed' in block letters. She stood there staring at the board. She had this feeling that it was not closed.

"We've solved the case. Let it go, Mattsen," said Gomez,

"It's open-and-shut. She tried to kill him, and karma took care of her. It's a textbook case of a relationship homicide. In most cases, it's always one of the pair and sometimes a lover. The motive was there—she wanted it all. But, Mrs. Appleton, in her haste to cover up and stop the bomb from exploding, forgot she was not supposed to pick it up."

Vikki turned to him. "What did Rinkin say she said when she opened the closet?"

"I can't remember his exact words, but it seemed like she was surprised."

"Yes, so she was surprised. Maybe the bomb had been tampered with? Maybe she noticed it was different? She said, *'what the'*, grabbed it, and activated it."

Gomez shrugged. "It's plausible, but who could have done that? All that talk of pinball makes me want to play. It's been a while. Let's join them."

"No way. I'd rather go home and soak in the tub than pull a plunger and watch a ball ping off various obstacles as it—" Vikki stopped.

"What?

"As it rolled down," she said quietly. "Like a cellphone pinging off cell towers around it as the owner makes calls." She turned to Gomez, excited. "We'll have to contact cell phone providers. Find any familiar numbers that pinged off the tower closest to the cabin last night. Any of our suspects who were there last night is our killer."

Gomez nodded. "I know who to call."

CHAPTER TWENTY-SIX

Vikki stopped at the wrought-iron gate and pushed the intercom. She was about to try again when the butler's voice, hoarse with sleep, came through.

"Yes."

"Detective Mattsen and Gomez here to see Mr. Appleton."

"Mr. Appleton has retired for the night. Can you come back tomorrow?"

"No, can do," Vikki said. "Mr. Smith, please open the gate, or we will climb over. Kindly inform Mr. Appleton we are on our way."

The gate swung open.

Vikki gunned the engine of her white Explorer up the hill. Behind her, Gomez and two officers followed in a police cruiser.

The butler, his eyes red from sleep, let them in. "Mr. Appleton will be with—"

Mr. Appleton walking into the living room, securing the belt of a red silk dressing gown around his waist. "Stay right there, Paul, so you can let them out. This is going to be short."

Paul nodded.

Mr. Appleton turned to Vikki and Gomez. "Detectives—it's eleven p.m. This better be good. I find it hard to fall asleep and impossible to continue when woken up like this."

Vikki leaned forward. "You were right, sir, your wife was having an affair."

Preston shrugged. "I suspected, but I had to get evidence. I didn't become a multi-millionaire by being stupid. I have an iron-clad prenup, but any attorney worth his salt could rip chunks out of it if we went to court. Having evidence would give me a better chance."

Vikki nodded.

Preston turned to Gomez and raised both hands. "Most of this will go to a trust after I die, and not to philandering bimbo. Don't tell me you woke me up just to remind me of what I already know."

"No," Gomez said. "We know you told Eve you were going to Boston, and we confirmed you were in Boston on Sunday night. You are a fortunate man."

Vikki let out a breath. "Mr. Appleton, your wife did want to kill you, and that trip to Boston saved your life. She had planted a pressure cooker bomb in the closet where you placed your fishing gear. She would have activated the bomb when you went fishing and blown you up."

Mr. Appleton stared at them, his eyes as wide as saucers.

Beside him, the butler, eyes swiveling, went utterly still.

"Since you were out of town," Gomez said, "she had to deactivate the bomb. Someone had gotten there before her, tampered with it, and changed the activating device to a motion trigger with a few seconds' delay."

"But still," said Mr. Appleton, "You could have told me all this in the morning."

Vikki nodded. "We recovered fingerprints from the device. Our friends at the FBI did us a favor. Rushed it through the Integrated Automated Fingerprint Identification System (IAFIS). We found a match."

Preston swallowed. His eyes darted from Gomez to Mattsen, then to the door. "Whose prints?"

Vikki stood alert. "We looked at phone numbers that pinged off cell towers closest to your cabin on Sunday."

Gomez approached Mr. Appleton—his jacket open, right hand dangling by his side.

"Only one was where it shouldn't be—Paul Smith's. The first time we came here, Mr. Smith assured us he wasn't at the cabin."

Preston gasped. "My God, Paul! What did you do?"

Vikki reached behind her for her cuffs. "Mr. Paul Smith, interlock your fingers behind your head. You're under arrest for the murder of Eve Appleton. Anything you—"

Mr. Smith bolted for the door.

"Shit." Vikki dashed after him.

Mr. Smith hadn't gone far. He was walking back into the room, his hands in the air. In front of him was one of the uniforms pointing a gun at him.

Vikki unhooked her cuffs. "Good job." She read him his Miranda rights as she cuffed him.

Mr. Appleton glanced at his butler and couldn't hide his disappointment. "Why, Paul, why?"

"Because I've been with you for thirty years, sir," Mr. Smith said. "She...she planned to kill you and inherit all your money. I overheard her on her cellphone, so I went to the cabin." His cockney accent made an appearance. "She's nothing but a cunt and a gold digger. And I knew she would cut me out of your will. Out of everything I had worked so hard for."

Mr. Appleton shook his head. "You should have told me."

CHAPTER TWENTY-SEVEN

Later the following day, a man in Bermuda shorts and a shirt sat in the departure lounge at terminal C of Newark Liberty. Even though it was just five-thirty a.m., dark sunglasses covered his eyes with a baseball cap throwing a shadow across his face.

Around him were other passengers in similar outfits. It was obvious their destination was a warm place with lots of beaches.

The smell of coffee from the Starbucks kiosk wafted through the air. He was tempted to get a cup but decided to wait until he was safely in the air.

A woman in the airline blue uniform and a *don't talk to me* expression walked toward the counter. The *click-click-click* of her stilettos shattered the early morning serenity. She dropped her handbag behind the counter and threw open the tunnel entrance to the plane.

Watching her, the man felt like a weight had been lifted off his shoulders—boarding would begin soon. He took a deep breath as he stretched out. Soon, he would be in Brazil. His phone chirped.

He froze.

Anyone watching would think he was practicing the posture of Christ the Redeemer in preparation to seeing the real statue in Rio de Janeiro. His stomach churned. A bitter taste flooded his mouth. The only person who knew that number was Eve.

Hands shaking, he dug into his shirt pocket and took out the phone. The screen said SIPD.

His right foot tapped the floor of its own accord. Compelled by some unknown force, he looked up—two familiar faces approached. A comforting, warm sensation originated below the belt, and he felt dampness.

"Going somewhere in a hurry, Adam?" Vikki Mattsen said, putting away her phone.

Rinkin opened his mouth, then closed it without saying anything.

Gomez sniffed the air. "Is that piss I smell?" He reached behind him and pulled out his cuffs. "Mr. Adam Rinkin, you are now under arrest for conspiracy to murder Preston Appleton. Anything..."

CHAPTER TWENTY-EIGHT

"Wow, that was a crazy case," said Ted. "So, they found the butler's fingerprint on the black piece of material you recovered at the scene?"

Vikki sighed. She was still floating from the sex afterglow. "It was a piece of the handle to the cooker. The butler overheard Mrs. Appleton and Rinkin talking about the bomb and the plot to kill Appleton. So, he went—rejigged the bomb to a motion trigger with a five-second delay."

"But he's only a butler. What does he know about electronics?"

"We dug up his records," Vikki said. "Before working for Mr. Appleton, he was in the British army as a young man and was trained in ordinances. The first time we met Mr. Appleton, he mentioned he was well versed in hand-to-hand combat."

Ted sighed. "And he had a million dollars coming to him from Mr. Appleton's estate in his will."

"Yep."

"I wouldn't let a million dollars' inheritance walk away from me just like that. I would have done something."

Vikki cocked her head. "Murder?"

Ted shook his head. "As Mr. Appleton said, he should have come to him." He was on his elbow, his palm flat on her stomach. His eyes bore into hers.

She was naked and felt like he was seeing into her mind. There were things locked behind her eyes and her mind she didn't want him to see. She shut them.

"Rinkin was abandoning his family?"

"He's just another sleazy guy. I don't know how Eve convinced him to go along with murdering her husband."

Ted's fingers shimmied down, massaging everything in their path.

Vikki laughed.

"The power of persuasion. It's tough for a man to say no to a relentless, determined, confident, beautiful woman. Who is rich."

Her eyes flashed open. A smile tugged the corner of her lips. "You think I'm pretty?"

He held her chin and rolled her face from side to side. "Nope, just confident and determined." He nodded. "Well, the face has potential. Too serious, though. A smile wouldn't hurt. Come on, smile for me."

Vikki couldn't help herself—she smiled. Then she traced a finger from his stomach and down. He rose to the occasion.

Ted sighed. "I'm so glad I met you. I wish this would go on forever. But I have to go."

"It's already beaten all the other records. By the way, what size of shoes do you wear?"

Ted raised an eyebrow. "Why?" He looked over at his loafers on the floor. "Is something wrong with my shoes? I thought it was only Gomez who had a shoe fetish. The day he dropped me off, he kept asking for my shoe size."

"No, I was testing a hypothesis. Never mind." Vikki's voice trailed off.

. . .

The End

ABOUT THE AUTHOR

Ifeanyi Esimai is a mystery and crime writer and enjoys reading across different genres. When he's not writing or reading, he's exploring documentaries on museums and ancient history.

Click here or the image to get all ten books!

Get a FREE copy of The Rookie!

Join my reader group for updates, giveaways, teasers, and a FREE copy of the prequel - The Rookie. Click here or scan the QR code

Prologue

She was all over him like a vulture circling a dying animal —something was up, but he couldn't put a finger on it.

"I'll shower, then we'll do it," she said. Her voice was a sexy purr. She shed the last of her clothing and headed for the bathroom.

He didn't want to look, but it had a magnetic attraction. Her jet-black hair fell to the middle of her back against golden tanned skin. Her legs went on forever. His eyes were glued to her heart-shaped ass—the eighth wonder of the world.

She disappeared into the bathroom. The shower came on, and she sang. Maybe this was his opportunity to bail. The room swayed. His head throbbed, signaling the beginning of a headache. Was it the vodka? It'd tasted a little different—some strong Russian shit. He shook his head. The room stopped moving.

He didn't want to 'do it.' How should he remove himself? Feign tiredness? Or say he had some disease?

The thought of a disease and his penis falling off made his balls retreat, mirroring a turtle's withdrawal into its shell.

Good.

Now, which disease should he tell her? HIV? Syphilis? Gonorrhea? Maybe ticks. He had a sudden breakthrough—COVID! Dick Covid. That could be a movie star's name. He was lost in his thoughts when the bathroom door burst open. She sauntered in—wet, naked, and ready.

She was a leopard about to pounce on its prey. "I love your dreamy eyes."

He saw an opening—to say he was tired. "I don't think—"

She threw her arms around his neck. The smell of wildflowers and vanilla filled his nostrils.

She leaned close to his ear and said, "Sweetheart, I need you right now." Her voice was a whisper. Her breath, pure heat against his skin. She nibbled on his earlobe, then traced a wet path down his neck.

All the self-affirmation he'd given himself minutes earlier flew out of the window. There was no escape. He was a man, after all. He went from zero to steel in milliseconds.

Maybe, just this once.

Her fingers did a quick work of his belt and zipper. His jeans fell, bunched up around his ankles.

"God." The word shuddered out of him.

She shoved him, and he fell onto the bed. She crawled on top of him, kissing his forehead, cheeks, and lips. She guided him inside her, enveloping him with her warmth.

He moaned. They were off to the races.

She rose and fell at a furious pace—no doubt who was in control. Her lovemaking was always on steroids as she chased another release.

After she finished with him, he felt as if he'd survived eight rounds with Mike Tyson in the ring.

"Now, let's go and relax in the hot tub." She helped him up.

It didn't look like sleep was on her agenda. He didn't want to move but didn't want to make her suspicious. The sex was good, but there was a type of clarity one attains after an orgasm. He must get away from her before it was too late.

She opened the sliding door, and he stumbled along.

The warm air outside felt good on his naked skin. He looked up and took a deep breath. The night sky was full of stars. The blinking light of a plane cut across the sky.

She led him to the tub. "Ah, always ready for me. Now sit. Don't go anywhere. I'll be right back."

He climbed on. The tub wobbled, and he held the sides for support. He'd spend the night. In the morning, he'd be out of here for good. He could not be a part of this.

"Ah." He let out a sigh. The water was warm. The sprays and jets were soothing and caressing. A worthwhile alternative to a Masseuse. He felt sleepy. The sound of splashing waves generated in the tub didn't help—a lullaby. He blinked repeatedly, trying to keep his eyes open.

"Here you go." She handed him a wine glass filled to the brim with a clear liquid. She sat next to him. "Cheers."

He lifted his glass and sniffed—more vodka. "Thank you." He took a sip. It tasted like the last one—bitter. Scared he might drop it, he downed it in one gulp and placed the empty glass on the edge of the tub. He relaxed, both arms stretched out on the side of the tub.

She traced circles on his chest and nibbled his ear. "Have I told you today how wonderful you make me feel?" Her voice was sexy and seductive. "You are a miracle worker."

His eyes fluttered. He needed a miracle to keep them open. "You are the miracle worker," he said. But no words came out. It was all in his head. His vision became foggy. He slid down the tub.

She giggled. "What are you doing?"

The water climbed up his face—chin, mouth, nose. He held his breath. The water stung his eyes. He tried to raise his head. His body refused to obey him. His heart raced. He had the sensation of being smothered. Yet, his body refused to move.

Water went over his head, a gurgling sound bubbling in his ears. He needed air.

That was his last conscious thought.

Chapter 1

Vikki sprang off the bed with a suddenness reminiscent of a Jack-in-the-box. The bed springs groaned.

"Where are you going?" Ted said.

"Time to go." She picked up her panties, bra, jeans, and t-shirt and headed for the bathroom. She tinkled and dressed quickly. She'd take a bath when she got to her place.

"I have to go. It was a pleasure knowing you."

He opened his mouth...[click here for next in series]